Kids love re
Choose Your Own

> It's like a video game the way the book is set up. Also it has so many endings that it's like you saved a spot in the game and went back.

Deacon Garcia-DeForge, age 10

> I love how you can go back once you get to the end! There is so much suspense!

Lily Weigand, age 10

> I read them because they really hook me into them and it gives you choices. That way it takes you on an adventure and you don't have to read page to page.

Alannah Audet, age 11

> Sometimes you can't get sucked into a good book but these are amazing :)

Kaiden Vernile, age 12

> These books are so fun! You always have a choice, but sometimes you can make a winning choice but if you make the wrong choice you're a goner.

Alexis Bador, age 11

CHOOSE YOUR OWN ADVENTURE®

TIME TRAVEL INN

BY BART KING

ILLUSTRATED BY MARÍA PESADO

CHOOSECO®
WAITSFIELD, VERMONT

For information regarding permission, write to:

CHOOSECO
P.O. Box 46
Waitsfield, Vermont 05673
www.cyoa.com

Publisher's Cataloging-In-Publication Data
(Prepared by The Donohue Group, Inc.)
Names: King, Bart, 1962- author. | Pesado, Maria, illustrator.
Title: Time Travel Inn / by Bart King ; illustrated by Maria Pesado.
Other Titles: Choose your own adventure.
Description: Waitsfield, Vermont : Chooseco, [2021] | Interest age level: 010-013. | Summary: "No one seems very worried that your Grandmother Dolores has vanished from her job as innkeeper in the middle of the Wisconsin woods. That is until your parents suddenly and mysteriously insist on moving the family to take over the inn while she's 'away.' Kids in the neighborhood are eager to tell you wild tales about your new home, the Time Travel Inn. In this longer, larger-format Choose Your Own Adventure ... kids can travel the past, present, and future as they make choices that lead to multiple thrilling outcomes while travelin' in search of Grandma Dolores."--Provided by publisher.
Identifiers: ISBN 9781937133771
Subjects: LCSH: Taverns (Inns)--Wisconsin--Juvenile fiction. | Time travel--Juvenile fiction. | Missing persons--Wisconsin--Juvenile fiction. | Grandmothers--Juvenile fiction. | CYAC: Hotels, motels, etc.--Fiction. | Time travel--Fiction. | Missing persons--Wisconsin--Fiction. | Grandmothers--Fiction. | LCGFT: Fantasy fiction. | Choose-your-own stories.
Classification: LCC PZ7.1.K585 Ti 2021 | DDC [Fic]--dc23

Published simultaneously in the United States and Canada

Printed in Canada

10 9 8 7 6 5 4 3 2 1

To Mrs. Shaw:
Thank you for encouraging all of your students,
and for teaching us the power of imagination.

BEWARE and WARNING!

This book is different from other books.

YOU and you alone are in charge of what happens in this story.

There are dangers, choices, adventures, and consequences. YOU must use all of your numerous talents and much of your enormous intelligence. The wrong decision could end in disaster—even death. But don't despair. At any time, YOU can go back and make another choice, alter the path of your story, and change its result.

You and your parents have recently moved from Florida to Wisconsin, to take over running the family inn while your Grandmother Dolores is "away." The only problem is, she vanished without a trace several years ago, and you think the Time Travel Inn might have something to do with her disappearance. When you and your new friends start to unravel the mysteries of the inn, will you be able to travel through time successfully to find your grandmother? Or will you be impaled by a gladiator or eaten by a velociraptor before you get the chance? You decide. . . Good luck!

You lean your head on the window of the passenger side of your dad's van and sigh. It's been a long car ride from Florida to Wisconsin, and it's gotten colder and more terrible each hour of the trip. Snowflakes are falling faster and faster, and then you see the sign:

"We're here!" announces Dad as he parks. You've finally reached your missing grandmother's motel in Wisconsin. The place doesn't look like much. You can see a lobby attached to the front of the innkeeper's house. *Your* house, you mentally correct yourself. There are also a bunch of guest rooms connected by an outdoor walkway. These rooms all face the parking lot, where two boys are shooting baskets at a shortened basketball hoop mounted on the side of the inn's roof.

It sure doesn't look like home.

You and Dad get out of the moving van, and it's so cold, it takes your breath away.

I already don't like it here, you think. You were sorry to hear Grandmother Dolores went missing, but you still don't understand why your family had to *move* to this Wisconsin motel of hers. Sure, you love her, but it's always been a long-distance relationship.

"Hey, guys," Dad calls. One of the boys waves and smiles. He's wearing a jacket with a big deer head on the front.

You ignore them and walk toward the inn's lobby. Outside is a sandwich board reading, "OPENING SOON!" Inside, there are old paintings and lots of bookshelves. A TV plays a history channel, and there is a huge eagle head mounted on the wall. Its eyes seem to follow you.

"Mom?" you call out.

Crickets.

That is, all you hear *is* crickets. From the noise they're making, they must be big ones.

Turn to page 3.

光
DAD JOKES
Bart King

Dad pokes his head into the lobby.

"Mom's not here?" Dad asks you, looking around. "She must be cleaning one of the rooms. Why don't you make some new friends?"

Dad walks away through the walkway. You frown in annoyance. Your dad always assumes you and everyone else are as friendly as he is.

But you go back outside, and the boy wearing the deer jacket comes over to you.

"Hi, I'm Damien, and this is Trent. Want to shoot some hoops?"

"She probably doesn't even *play* basketball," says Trent, ignoring you.

"I'm Astrid. I just moved here from Florida." You lunge and steal the basketball from Trent. Then you dribble twice and slam dunk. "It's 1–0. Your ball."

"That was a foul," complains Trent. Damien just laughs and says, "Hold up." He unzips the legs off his camo pants. After stepping out of the pant legs, he's wearing camo shorts. "Okay, I'm ready!"

Trent inbounds the ball to Damien, who gives you a silly head-fake and then shoots. The ball launches way over the basket, bounces on the inn's roof, and rolls behind the backboard.

It's stuck there.

Turn to page 6.

Inn

"Sorry! Now we need a ladder," says Damien. "Astrid, you probably don't know this, but the Time Travel Inn is a legend around here. This place has been run down for ages, but people talk about how weird things sometimes—"

"Astrid!" Dad shouts. "Come quick!"

You look around. "Dad?" you shout back as the snow begins falling harder. "Where are you?"

There is no reply.

"He's probably lost already," says Trent.

You hear a distant phone ring. You race back into the lobby, where the telephone on the inn's check-in counter is ringing. You pick it up and hear your mother's voice. "Astrid, is that you? I want you to promise me to stay out of the basement—"

"Mom? Hello?" you ask, but the line goes dead. Annoyed and a little scared, you step behind the counter. A door opens to a family room with a sofa and TV. A hallway leads off the family room. This must be the inn's residence—your new home.

"Hello? Mom? Dad, are you here?" you yell down the hallway and into the residence.

There is no answer.

Go on to the next page.

Damien and Trent followed you, and now the boys look at you with wide eyes.

"Who was it?" Damien asks.

"My mom," you explain. "She said to stay out of the basement, and then the line went dead."

Trent whistles. "Spooky stuff, Astrid!" he says, and starts messing with some of the curiosities on the lobby shelves.

You shut your eyes for a second. You need to think. A few months ago, your parents dropped two huge surprises on you. The first surprise was that your grandmother was feared dead.

Grandmother Dolores had been a scientist for the U.S. government. After a scandal with her experiments, she either quit or was fired. You never got the full story from your parents.

Grandmother Dolores moved to Wisconsin and bought the Time Travel Inn. She still did projects for the government, and was always traveling and very busy. So you had only seen Grandmother in person a few times in your life before she vanished.

A few years ago, Grandmother didn't return from one of her trips. Your parents hadn't worried at first, because she often traveled to remote places. But eventually they realized Grandmother wasn't on a normal trip. Your parents tried everything they could think of, but she'd had no contact with anyone. Even a private investigator could not track your grandmother down.

Last month, she'd been declared legally "dead." And so your parents had inherited Grandmother Dolores's estate.

The second surprise came when Mom quit her job as a history professor and told you the whole family was moving to Wisconsin to take over the Time Travel Inn! When you asked why, your parents talked about how it was always a dream of theirs, and it was time for a change in scenery.

Turn to the next page.

The whole thing didn't make any sense. And now here you are in a strange place with no friends . . . and now no parents, either.

You see a key hanging on a hook. The key has a sticker on it reading "Master." You put the key in your pocket and look around the lobby for anything else useful. You notice an old book that's open on the check-in counter. Its pages are covered in delicate handwriting. Maybe there's a clue in there, but it would take a lot of reading to find out.

"Sorry about this, guys," you say to Trent and Damien, "but I think you should go home so I can get to the bottom of this. I just need to decide—"

A deep voice interrupts:

"LEAVE THIS ROOM TO AVOID YOUR DOOM."

"Who's there?" you gasp.

Trent looks ready to bolt out the door, but Damien is grinning.

"That was SO wild!" he says, as if the voice of doom just wished him a happy birthday.

As you look carefully around, this time you see the giant eagle's beak open as it says:

"MAKE HASTE! FOR TIME IS NOT YOURS TO WASTE."

Go on to the next page.

You stare at the huge eagle head in disbelief, and then you and the boys start peppering it with questions:

"Hello? Say something else!"

"Who are you?"

"What did you mean?"

"Do you have any money?"

"Why are bald eagles 'bald' if they have head feathers?"

But the eagle is silent.

"It must be a robot," Trent says. "And the message is recorded. My dad has a fish like that, and it sings rock songs."

"That settles it," says Damien. "We aren't going anywhere. Instead, Trent and I are going to help you find your parents. Where do you want to look?"

You're secretly glad they aren't leaving. "Thanks. The last I saw him, Dad was walking toward the back of the inn. And on the phone just now, Mom said to stay out of the basement."

Trent is snooping around the lobby. "I bet the basement is below this residence part of the motel, not the guest rooms. My parents say there was something weird about the way the place was built, though, so it could be anywhere. Everything about this place is weird. And *everyone*," he adds.

You sigh. Trent obviously means *you*. But you won't rise to the bait. Should you go into your new home and try to find the basement, or avoid it like your Mom told you? Maybe you can find more clues in this weird lobby.

If you stay out of the basement and keep looking here, turn to the next page.

If you decide to find the basement and see if your dad is there, turn to page 15.

10

Your mom told you to stay out of the basement, and you decide you'll listen. You see that the phone on the lobby counter has a sticky note taped to it that reads, "Press 9 to Page."

You lift the receiver, push nine, and talk: "Mom, Dad, this is Astrid." You can hear your voice echoing on distant speakers. Wherever your parents are, they should be able to hear you. "Please call me back at the front lobby!"

You hang up and cross your fingers for luck. As you wait for a call back, you look more carefully at the old book on the counter. It has no title, and the pages are handwritten. At the top of the page is a date from 60 years ago.

"Hey you guys, listen to this from this old diary." You read aloud:

> Here in these woods, I'll continue the "dangerous research" that led to my removal at DARPA. My theory was simple: With the right technology, an object can move between different points in time. But my results were complicated, and led to me fleeing from a carnivorous reptile of surprising size —.

You skim ahead. "It sounds like someone was writing a science fiction story."

"Or working on a time machine," says Trent.

Go on to the next page.

"Hey, that person worked for DARPA?" asks Damien. "I did a social studies report on that! It stands for the Defense Advanced Research Projects Agency. So whoever wrote that must've been a real techno-geek."

You reach the end of the diary's first entry, and at the bottom is a signature:

Dolores Alcindor

This is your grandmother's diary!

"You guys," you say breathlessly, "my grandmother used to work at DARPA, and she wrote this." You keep reading aloud: "'I believe that with some simple adjustments, guests at the Time Travel Inn will be able to move safely in time. Of course, the cost will be high—'"

Trent interrupts with a laugh. "Sounds like your grandmother believed in magic."

"Hey, be cool," says Damien. "Remember, people used to think rainbows were magic until we figured out they are raindrops in the air getting hit by sunlight." He pulls a tennis ball out of his coat pocket and tosses it in the air.

"Rainbows *aren't* magic?" asks Trent sarcastically. "So I suppose leprechauns and centaurs are fake too, right?" He cups his hands: "Throw the ball here."

Damien tosses the tennis ball to Trent, who drops it, and the ball rolls off toward a couch.

"You guys?" Trent squeaks. "*Look*." He points at the couch.

Turn to the next page.

You all look to the couch. Damien's tennis ball is being rolled back and forth by a giant cricket. It must be eighteen inches long, and it's looking at the ball like it could be food. The cricket then glances up and locks eyes directly with *you*.

Damien whispers, "Um, Astrid, I know bugs are bigger in Florida. Is that thing yours?"

"Yes," you say sarcastically. "I brought a giant cricket along to help me unpack my stuff."

The cricket cocks its head and rolls the ball to Damien. He nudges the ball back to the cricket with his sneaker.

You notice a piece of paper tied to the cricket's body. It looks like it has writing on it. It might be a clue to what's going on here.

"Hey, big fella," you say softly, raising your hands to be nonthreatening. The cricket looks at you curiously and doesn't seem afraid. "What do you have there?"

"Dude, be careful," warns Trent. "It's probably a carnivore."

Turn to page 14.

At that moment, the wind gusts outside. The sandwich board falls over and hits the lobby window with a *BANG*!

Startled, the giant cricket leaps high over your heads. As the three of you duck, it lands gracefully on the lobby counter and then disappears into the family room behind it.

You follow, grabbing the old leather book off the counter as you go in case you need a weapon. You step into the family room with Trent and Damien right behind you. There are two doors off the room. One goes into the residence hallway, and the other one leads outside. This door is ajar, and you see the giant cricket squeeze through the door and outside, into the snow.

You push the door to the outside wide open, and snowflakes and cold air rush to meet your face. From here, you can see the Time Travel Inn's front parking lot. The inn's rooms are next to it, so guests can park and then walk beneath the overhang.

The snow is falling thick and heavy, and some has blown in under the covered walkway, covering the cricket's trail. You take a few steps and the boys follow, but you see no sign of the huge insect.

"There it is!" says Damien, pointing.

The cricket is out in the snow, jumping around and looking up at the flakes as if it's never seen snow before.

"Stupid bug, it's going to freeze if it stays there," says Trent. "But before that freak of nature turns into a cricket ice cube, maybe we can sell it to a museum or something. Let's capture it!"

How cruel! you think. *But maybe there's a way for us to save that cricket before it freezes.*

"Maybe we could convince it to go into one of the rooms," Damien suggests. "Didn't you take the master key?" he asks you.

If you agree with Damien and unlock a motel room to lure the cricket out of the cold, turn to page 18.

If you go with Trent's idea and try to catch the cricket, go to page 70.

"I'm going to look in the basement," you say. "Follow me if you want to live."

When the two boys look at you like you're a maniac, you add, "I'm joking about that last part, guys."

You close the leather book and walk down the hallway to the residence. As you do, the hallway seems to extend farther than it should, making you feel a little dizzy. You shake the feeling away. Is it just the cold Wisconsin air, so different from the Florida temperatures you're used to?

"Let's split up," you say. "I'll look on the right side of the hall, you two do the left."

"But that's a classic horror movie mistake!" Damien protests.

"C'mon, this isn't a horror movie," you say. "We're just three kids looking for my parents. And a ladder. In a deserted motel during a snowstorm." But the more you say, the worse it sounds, so you step through the first doorway you find.

Mom set up an office in this room. There are boxes and files arranged carefully and a desk with neat piles of papers. As you look through them, Damien's voice interrupts: "Hey Astrid, we found it!"

"I'll be right there!" you yell.

Turn to the next page.

16

You run down the hallway and find the boys in what must be your parents' bedroom. Damien stands inside the walk-in closet. He has shifted some luggage to reveal an open trapdoor.

"We had to move some things to find it," he says apologetically. As you look down the trapdoor, you see stairs leading into the darkness. Cold, stale air wafts up.

Something seems suspicious about this whole thing. Trent looks tense, but Damien is grinning. "This must have something to do with the construction that Trent's parents talked about!"

You call down the stairway: "Mom? Dad?"

Your words echo in the dark. Then a harsh voice answers: *"Begone, if you value your soul!"*

Trent and Damien both run to the bedroom door. "Th-that giant talking eagle was bad enough," Trent stammers. "But I'm drawing the line at someone shoplifting my soul! See you later, Astrid."

You wonder if you should try to persuade the boys to stay. But do you even need them? This is *your* family's inn, after all.

If you decide to go down the stairs by yourself, turn to page 22.

If you try to talk the boys into sticking around, turn to page 32.

18

The giant cricket watches as you unlock Room 1 with the master key. When you push its door open, warm air wafts out.

"Come on, big fella," encourages Damien. "Come inside and warm up."

The cricket shakes the snow off itself like a dog and hops obediently into the room. You start to follow it in, but stop short.

A triceratops stands in the room, facing you!

"What a realistic dinosaur model!" exclaims Damien. He rushes up to inspect the pony-sized triceratops. "I think this is a combo coat rack/ironing board," Damien announces, putting his hands on the flat part of the dino.

You look around and see that this is no ordinary motel room. It has a prehistoric theme.

"Your grandmother has really great taste in interior decoration," jokes Trent. "I wonder where she dug all *this* up?"

There are pictures on the walls that look like birds crossed with pterodactyls. In the corner there is a large, glass-topped display case. Inside it are old dried plants, pressed leaves, and a dead dragonfly the size of a crow.

You hear a chirp and see the giant cricket leap onto the desk, next to a gleaming machine.

Unafraid, Damien walks right up to the cricket. "Easy there. You're scared of us, aren't you . . . Davy?" He points to the note tied to the mammoth insect. "Hey, this guy's name is Davy Cricket. Says so right here."

The cricket chirps and jumps up on top of the device. It has a metal stamp reading "Chronometer Reversal Device," and buttons on the side. One button is marked "Power" and another is labeled "Landmass Adjuster." There is a digital readout that says: MESOZOIC.

Turn to page 20.

MESOZOIC
000,000,000

You remember from science class that the Mesozoic was an era from millions of years ago.

"What the heck? Is that thing supposed to be a time machine?" Trent asks.

"How cool would that be?" laughs Damien. "You could make a sequel to a time-travel movie that's released before the first film."

You shake your head. "I think this room just has a history theme. You know, like 'Indiana Jones, Dinosaur Hunter' or something. And I bet this fake time machine is part of the decoration."

You look around the room. The idea of the Time Travel Inn being set up like this strikes you as pure genius.

Go on to the next page.

Trent looks skeptical. "Let's find out if you're right about that, Nancy Drew," he says, reaching toward the device's power button.

"Don't," you say, picking up the chrome machine. It's surprisingly cold in your hands. "This is *my* family's inn, so if anyone is going to do anything with this thing, it's going to be ME."

Trent laughs. "So you actually DO think this might be a real time machine? What a joke. Now let me see it." He reaches and grabs the gleaming device back, and the two of you start a tug-of-war. As you do, the device suddenly lights up and Davy Cricket hops around excitedly.

"You guys, stop!" cries Damien. "Look, let's compromise. Just let me hold that thing for a minute and we can talk this out."

You hold tight to the device and glare at Trent. He has a stubborn expression, but if anyone can talk sense into him, it's Damien.

If you keep pulling on the device, turn to page 28.

If you agree to let Damien hold the machine, turn to page 180.

You look down the dark stairway. The last thing you want to do is to go down there alone, but you have to find your parents. The more time passes, the more you're sure they are in trouble.

"Listen," you say to the boys. "I appreciate you sticking with me as long as you did. But this is something I have to do alone."

You steel yourself and step down. As soon as your foot touches the first step, the harsh voice calls out: *"Fool! Turn back now, before it is too late."*

"Astrid, stop," implores Damien. "Why don't we call the police?"

"There's no time!" you reply, going down another step and reaching out for a light switch. There isn't one. The light shifts from dim to gloomy. Five steps down, it's getting really dark.

You freeze on the next step as the voice sounds again, louder this time: *"This is your final warning! Continue, and you will be a story that people tell around a campfire to frighten each other."*

"Mom?" you call quietly. "Dad?"

No reply.

Go on to the next page.

After twenty steps it's pitch black—and finally, your fingers find a switch. You flick it, and lights blaze on. And not just lights. Power thrums, and the sound of long-slumbering machines whirring into action fills the air.

You look around for the person who was threatening you, but instead you see something that makes you think: *This is officially the weirdest day of my life*.

"What's down there?" calls Damien.

"You wouldn't believe me if I told you," you reply. "Come on."

You hear Damien take a step onto the stairway above. As he does, a voice comes from a speaker on a wall: *"Fool! Turn back now, before it is too late."*

"That voice is from a security system," you call up.

Damien and Trent rush down the stairs and freeze at the bottom. In front of them is a wall of blinking electrical panels. From this wall, thick cables run to the object that all three of you are staring at.

Turn to the next page.

A miniature two-seater airplane stands in the middle of the basement floor, with nothing else around it.

"What the heck? It's an old kiddie ride," says Trent. "I can even see where the coins go. It's fifty cents a ride."

You get in the pilot's seat, and as you do, a woman's voice comes through the plane's dashboard: "Be sure to read instructions before initiating travel."

There is a steering wheel in front of you, next to a dashboard with a huge dial labeled "DD," and a glove box. You open the glove box and find an old, typed manual. Laying it across the steering wheel, you read:

EZ Operating Instructions for the Multi-Dimensional,
Dual-Channel Vortex Ingress Generator

You turn to the first page:

> "Introduction: My research in these woods has led me to the staggering finding that our world is just one of *many* universes. Some are nearly identical to ours, and some are dramatically different. Together, these multiple universes make up the multiverse. To test and explore my findings, I've invented a device leading from our Earth (Earth-1) to nearby ones. The idea for it came to me when I saw a child's airplane ride in front of a local supermarket . . ."

Turn to page 26.

You notice a signature at the bottom of this page:

Dolores Alcindor

Looking around the secret basement, you begin to understand. "Listen, you guys! My grandmother invented and built everything here. And she used this kiddie airplane to somehow get to other worlds in the multiverse. If my parents followed her, they might need my help."

Damien gets into the seat next to you. "They might need *our* help, you mean. I don't have to be home till dinnertime. Plus, if this works, we'll be the first people to ever visit another universe!"

"At best, we'd be the *second* people," corrects Trent.

Damien looks disappointed. "Dang, nobody remembers second place. I mean, who was the second person to walk on the Moon?"

You look at him. "Buzz Aldrin."

"Oh. Who was first?"

"Neil Armstrong," you sigh.

Go on to the next page.

Trent laughs. "You two look ridiculous on that thing. What's it called, anyway? Because right now, it looks like a Nerd-Mobile."

You read from the manual's introduction: "My device is called the Multi-Dimensional, Dual-Channel Vortex Ingress Generator (MDDCVIG). But I've nicknamed it the Doggy Door (DD). Its basic control is a dial, set to a baseline of Earth-1. Clicking on the dial can lead one to places like our present world, while others are far more exotic."

You turn the page and see a Table of Contents:

Getting Started

- Securing Your Environment
- Moving Sideways
- Avoiding Untimely Death (and Other Inconveniences)
- Language and Culture
- Artifacts
- Troubleshooting and FAQs
- Customer Support (There is no customer support at this time.)

Damien fishes in his pocket and takes out two quarters. "Let's go for a ride!"

You hear a noise from the top of the stairway. A strange man's voice whispers: "We need to hurry and stop them NOW."

Whoever is up there wants to stop you from activating the Doggy Door. That makes you want to use it, but you also want to know who is up there.

If you decide to use the Doggy Door right now, turn to page 38.

If you stop and go upstairs to see who is there, turn to page 104.

"Give it *here!*" you command, pulling on the gleaming device with all your might.

It pops right out of Trent's hands. You stagger back in victory, and Trent says, "I totally let go of it. Hey, what the heck?"

The crystals on the machine change color. It gives off a low thrum, and Davy Cricket jumps up and down, waving his antennae excitedly. Then the whole room ripples. Shocked, you reach to try to turn off the device, but its thrum gets louder.

And then you're falling through the air. You let go of the device and your eyes shut instinctively.

Is this a dream? you wonder. But the air is hot and humid, so you force them open and—

SPLASH!

You're underwater! Flailing your arms, you rise up and break the surface of the water, gasping. You hear a voice from behind you.

You turn and see Damien, bobbing in the water like a cork. The giant cricket is perched on his shoulder, avoiding the water like a cat. "I said, 'That was fun!'" Damien yells. "But what happened?"

You open your mouth to answer, but warm saltwater gets in, and you sputter instead.

Turn to page 30.

Catching your breath, you look around. Behind Damien and Davy, you can see Trent bobbing up and down. The water is clear and blue, like in the tropics. About 100 yards away, a long, supple tree trunk rises about fifteen feet from the water. Then the tree trunk turns toward you, and you realize it's a *neck*. It has a head with teeth that you can see even at this distance.

"Plesiosaur!" shouts Damien.

"Stop yelling!" Trent shouts back.

Apparently, the first rule of time travel is: you have to yell about every little thing. Or *gigantic* thing in the water, in this case.

You kick through the water toward a beach.

"Follow me!" you shout, and paddle fast. Damien swims next to you, and the cricket jumps onto your neck. You don't love that, but you're too busy trying not to get eaten by a sea dinosaur to complain.

You soon feel sand under your feet. As you and Damien run through the surf to the beach, you turn to check on Trent. He's stumbling in the surf—and the plesiosaur is right behind him!

If you go back into the water to help Trent, turn to page 42.

If you yell to warn Trent, turn to page 116.

"The Jabberwock approaches," says Nanoc grimly, like that explains everything.

"The Jabberwock . . . approaches?" repeats Trent.

"You know the poem from *Through the Looking-Glass*? 'Beware the Jabberwock, my son! / The jaws that bite, the claws that catch!' No? What do they teach kids on your world?" asks Nanoc, exasperated. "I guess this one's on me. The only way to kill a Jabberwock is with a vorpal blade. Seek shelter, children, while I deal with this foe."

Nanoc unsheathes her sword. You and the boys race to the massive steel door. You knock while the awful burbling sound grows louder. As the faun slowly opens it, you rush inside, and there is a sound like *snicker-snack*.

Then Nanoc's blue head rolls through the doorway.

"Guess her blade wasn't vorpal enough," you say. "Close the door!"

The four of you slam the door shut. You throw its huge bolt just as something thumps into it, and the whole wall shudders. The faun shakes her fist at you. "'Don't disturb the Jabberwock'! How hard is it?" She sprints off down the hall.

You look at the plane. "Damien, tell me you have two quarters!"

He shakes his head, and there is another smash on the door.

If you try to escape on your own, turn to page 97.

If you follow the faun, turn to page 121.

Trent and Damien keep backing away from the trapdoor until they're in the hallway.

"C'mon guys, where's your sense of adventure?" you demand. "You told me there was something mysterious about this place. Well, now's our chance to solve the mystery!"

Damien thinks about it and walks back toward you. But then the harsh voice from the basement speaks again: *"Still here? Begone! This is your final warning."*

Both boys turn and run, their footsteps echoing down the hall. You roll your eyes but decide you should stick with them.

"I'll come back here by myself if we can't find my parents," you mutter to yourself.

Go on to the next page.

The three of you search the rest of the house. You don't find anyone, but Damien does spot a ladder in a small storage room, so you can at least get Trent's basketball down from the roof. As you pull the ladder from the room, Trent's cell phone rings.

"*Seriously*, Mom? Right now?" He hangs up. "I've got to go, because both my parents say this snowstorm's 'a doozy.'"

You nod. Since the parking lot is on the way, you follow the boys out, carrying the ladder. The snow is coming down thick as you set the ladder against the building. Damien holds it while you climb up and reach behind the backboard to grab the basketball.

"Toss it down!" Trent says. "Then I can get out of here."

You drop the ball to him, but the wet ball has gotten a little frozen. It slips right between Trent's hands and bonks him in the face. He falls backward in the fresh snow.

Turn to the next page.

"Sorry!" you say, coming down the ladder. "You *said* you had it."

Trent just stalks off, so you call out, "Thanks for coming over!" while Damien gives you an apologetic shrug.

"I better go home, too," he says. "Nice to meet you, Astrid."

As you go back inside to put the ladder away, your mother rushes up to you. Her sweater is torn and it looks like someone aimed a leaf blower at her hair. Before you can say anything, your mom hugs you.

"THERE you are, Astrid!" she murmurs in your ear. "I've been looking everywhere for you."

Dad walks in to join you. He's limping a little and has grass stains on his knees. He comes up and hugs you and your mom without saying a word.

Turn to page 36.

After they let go, you pepper your parents with questions.

"Dad, where *were* you this whole time? And Mom, why did you make that weird phone call to the lobby? And what the heck is going on with the basement in this place?! Someone down there threatened me and my friends!"

Your parents exchange a look, and Dad forces a laugh. "Oh, that 'Begone!' warning is just a recorded message that plays when someone stands at the top of the stairs. Grandmother Dolores put it in as a joke. Anyway, the basement stairs are dangerous, and you're not to go down there until we get them fixed."

Go on to the next page.

The answers to your other questions are just as evasive and general. So a few days later, you sneak into your parents' closet and find the trapdoor sealed shut with a heavy lock.

Two weeks later, workmen come. After a lot of sawing and hammering, the trapdoor is gone. The floor in the closet is totally smooth, as if there were never a trapdoor there at all.

You can never persuade your parents to speak of what happened that day. Even years later, you will always know that you missed something.

But what?

The End

You study the massive dial on the dashboard of the airplane. It looks like a giant combination to a school locker and is set at "Earth-1." You turn the dial a few notches, grab the two quarters from Damien's hand, and pop them into the coin slot. As the coins rattle down, you blink your eyes, and when you open them . . .

You are standing outside, in a forest. The air is warm and trees press closely around you. While this is obviously no longer a Wisconsin forest in the winter, there is something familiar about the place.

"Where ARE we?" asks Damien.

Trent points. "Ask him." You follow Trent's finger and see a young boy dressed in medieval clothes staring at you. Did he wander away from a nearby Renaissance Faire?

"Hey kid!" yells Trent. "Come here."

The boy steps closer. He's holding a long, polished stick with a pointed end. The boy ignores Trent and Damien, but stares at you intently.

"You come from a distant land," the boy says. "Have you arrived to take part in our war here in Zamora?"

"Um, good question?" you reply.

The boy frowns. He backs up a step and scratches the soil with his stick, then mutters something.

"What the heck?" says Damien. "I can't move!"

You try to turn and look at him but find that you are frozen in place. You can breathe and speak, but not move.

Turn to page 40.

"I am going to get a member of the Grey Council," says the boy. "Please stay quiet while I'm gone. You don't want to bring attention to yourselves." With that, he disappears into the woods.

"This stinks," says Trent. "I *really* have to pee."

"Let me help take your mind off it," volunteers Damien. "Right now, we're on another version of Earth that's in another universe, right? But how many versions are there? I did a report on this, and a scientist named Stephen Hawking said there is actually just a small range."

"Okay, so how many universes are there, smart guy?" demands Trent.

"Only seven or eight trillion!"

"So in another multiverse, maybe you're a good basketball player?" asks Trent.

"Oh, good one," says Damien admiringly. "But think about this: Is there a Trent and a Damien and an Astrid here on this world already? And if so, did we just somehow REPLACE them? Or will we see them and be like 'Whoa, dude, you look familiar'?"

It's actually a good question, you think. But behind you, in the distance, you can hear footsteps crackling the leaves on the forest floor.

"Shh, listen!" you whisper. "Someone is behind us."

If you yell for help, turn to page 103.

If you decide to stay quiet, turn to page 47.

As the Grey Council's wizards watch, you think of Florida and Wisconsin and the connection you feel to this new world.

"I feel most at home *here,* in Zamora," you say. "I will stay as your new queen."

"Me too!" exclaims Damien. "Except for the being queen part, I mean."

Lamonta traces sigils on the floor. A gleaming crown appears in the air above the empty throne.

Your mother's jaw drops. "But Astrid, I can't stay here with you. I have to go back to Wisconsin!"

You race to her and the two of you hug tightly. "I love you, Mom. You'll come back, right?" She agrees, and you wipe tears from your eyes, then walk over and sit on the throne. The crown gently descends upon your head, fitting perfectly. You feel magick rise within you, and turn to the Grey Council. "What's our first order of business?"

"Your coronation ceremony, Queen Astrid," says Lamonta. Trumpets peal, the doors of the Great Dome open, and people from the city stream in. They clap for you and then do a version of the wave. But instead of raising their arms, they bow at the waist to you.

Trent laughs. "This is dumb. Stop acting like a royal hotshot, Astrid."

You freeze him with just a look. "Mom, please take *him* with you. Now, Grey Council, how shall we get this city back on its feet?"

The End

You take a deep breath, then splash into the shallow surf.

Trent trips and falls forward. A small wave breaks on his back.

"Leave me!" he sputters. "Save yourselves!"

Behind him, the mammoth plesiosaur is close. Very close. You grab Trent's hoodie and pull backward, trying to force him to his feet. Trent crawls with you, coughing up water. The dinosaur's head seems as big as a buffalo as it stretches toward you, getting closer, closer . . .

Then its mammoth jaws snap shut on air, and you and Trent scramble safely farther up the shore.

Exhausted and wet, you lie back on the warm sand. In front of you, tropical blue water laps the shore, and the disappointed plesiosaur disappears into deeper waters. The air is hot and humid, and it seems thicker somehow. About 100 yards behind you is a wall of green.

It takes you a moment to realize it's a jungle. All of the plants and trees seem bigger and somehow more "alive" than what you're used to.

"Thanks, Astrid," says Trent. "But I totally had that situation handled."

Damien laughs. "Is that why you were all 'Save yourselves'?"

Go on to the next page.

You grin and say, "Anyway, I guess that device really *was* a time machine."

Trent holds up a bottle. "Yeah, but how does that explain this? I grabbed it by accident when I was crawling up the beach. Looks like there's a message inside." He hands the bottle to you.

"Probably someone asking for help," says Damien, dusting sand off his jacket.

You fish the note out. It has writing that looks like a kindergartener wrote it. "'If you're reading this, you're going to need help,'" you read aloud.

"Yeah, thanks for the warning, kid," says Trent, and he starts laughing, almost hysterically.

But you're not listening, because you just noticed some big lizards.

The closest one is sunning itself in the sand about thirty yards away. It's about eight feet long and has very short legs. The lizard watches you, then rolls over to all fours, and a yellow tongue flicks out of its mouth.

"Shh!" you say, but Trent's laughter has woken up the other napping lizards. They start rolling to their feet and walking slowly forward. Davy Cricket crawls up to Damien's shoulder and peeks at the lizards from behind him.

Turn to page 45.

"Those look like crocodylomorphs," says Damien, then he notices your look of surprise. "Look, I read a lot of dinosaur books when I was little, okay?"

"Whatever they are, let's get out of here," you reply. "With those little legs, they can't be very fast."

As you walk away backward from the crocodylomorphs, you try to understand what's happening.

Are these dinosaurs?

Where are you?

When are you?

The lizards follow, but they can waddle only so fast. You and the two boys go faster, but then the lizards rear up on their little back legs and start running after you like ostriches.

"Run!" you shout. The three of you sprint up the beach. You look back over your shoulder and see the dinosaur pack is gaining.

Within moments, you're surrounded. The lizards drop down again to all fours and start circling you. Now you can see that they have remarkably large teeth.

Damien whips off his jacket, revealing a camouflage fanny pack. He unzips it, rummages inside, and pulls out a small set of nunchucks. The dinosaurs continue circling, then one dashes at Damien from behind.

Turn to the next page.

"Look out!" you warn. Damien swings his tiny nunchucks and misses. The lizard retreats, but the rest of the reptiles press closer. The lizards look like they're all going to pounce at once, and you prepare to fight for your life—

"Hey, get out of there!" yells a child's voice. Amazingly, the big lizards scamper off into the jungle, and a six-year-old girl walks out of the jungle toward you.

"Wow, you speak dinosaur?" asks Damien.

"No, I speak English," the girl replies. She has on a name tag that reads "Faith" and is wearing a dog whistle around her neck. "Davy Cricket!" she exclaims, waving to Davy. "Hey, are you guys on a field trip too?"

More children appear, holding small spears and little homemade bows and arrows. They all wear name tags. While their clothes are a bit dirty, they seem healthy.

"Who are YOU?" demands Trent.

"This is our kindergarten class," says Faith. "You must be the new teacher's assistants! Come with us back to our camp, and we'll make you some name tags."

You think, *Babysitting a bunch of armed little kids? No thanks.* But you are also curious about who these children are and how they got to the age of dinosaurs. You look at Trent and Damien with your eyebrows raised, wondering what they think. They look as confused as you! You'd better decide what to do.

If you agree to travel with the children to their camp, turn to page 53.

If you decide to go your own way with Trent and Damien, turn to page 71.

You stay quiet and the footsteps fade away behind you. You study the shapes the boy scratched into the dirt. It's strange, but you can somehow *read* them. They make sense to you.

Perhaps an hour later, the boy returns with a tall woman who is also holding a long stick. She ignores Damien and Trent and stares piercingly at you.

"I see what you meant, Ando. This one is glowing," says the woman, gesturing at you. With her stick, she scratches a shape in the dirt, and you are able to move again. "What is your name, child?"

"Astrid," you reply. Then you add, "Mi lady," and Trent laughs.

"I am Lamonta of the Grey Council of Zamora. Are you a spy, Astrid? There is no other way you could have gotten past our defenses to arrive here."

Trent snorts. "*We* got here through a Doggy Door, of course. Now unfreeze me—"

Lamonta makes another sign in the dirt, and Trent's mouth shuts. "Follow me, Astrid," she says, walking away.

You don't move. "I'm not leaving without my friends."

Lamonta turns and raises an eyebrow. "These two have no magick, nor do they have any skill as warriors. My city is at war and can ill afford two more mouths to feed."

Turn to the next page.

Glancing down at the shapes drawn in the ground, you get an idea. You pick up a stick, add a line to one arc. Then you erase part of a shape. And because it somehow feels right, you say, "Dlorreg."

And with that, the two boys can move again!

"What the heck?" exclaims Damien. "Freezing someone by scratching dirt with a stick is against the basic laws of the universe!"

"Perhaps those laws are not as basic as you think," says Lamonta. "Now come."

The five of you walk quickly through the forest, and Damien mutters, "Maybe the laws are more like *suggestions*."

After a time, the trees thin out and you reach an immense city that looks like it was built during the Renaissance. At the city's center, you see a massive dome. But perhaps the most interesting thing about the city is the thick wall around it. It's nearly invisible!

"That's one weird wall," you say.

"What wall?" asks Trent.

A group of guards stands at an almost-transparent gate. They nod respectfully at Lamonta and stare at you. This same thing happens as your group walks down a street and heads for the dome.

Turn to page 50.

Lamonta and Ando lead your group into a building on the side of the dome. Once inside, they take you into a large library. Lamonta tells Ando to keep your group here for now.

"Wait one hour," Lamonta says to Ando. "Then bring them to the Grey Council."

Lamonta rushes from the library. The heavy door closes behind her and it sounds like a latch is thrown.

Damien tests the door. "Locked," he says.

You scan the library bookshelves. You are drawn to a book called *Sigils of Opening*. You take it down from the shelf and examine it.

Ando looks approvingly at your choice.

"A sigil is a symbol with magical power," Ando tells you.

You look through the book. Its pages have a bewildering combination of words, numbers, and symbols. They look like math equations. As you stare, the sigils seem to fall into place in a way that makes sense to you on a deep level.

You find a piece of heavy chalk on a desk, and begin drawing a diagram on the stone floor with your own symbols and lines. It looks and feels right. How do you know this?

Ando watches you with interest. "Your sigils are excellent," he says. "Are you trying to open the door?"

Go on to the next page.

"Yes." You pause and look up. "But how do I know how to do this? And who is Zamora fighting? And what started this war? Like, is this a good versus evil thing?"

Ando laughs. "Life is more complex than that." Then he gives you a long lecture about the history of magick in the world of Bellaquom. Centuries ago, the first spellcaster, a mathematician, realized that there was a deep power in magick. Humans learned how to tap into it. But as more people studied the new field, there was a split in the magick community.

"The Blue Wizards use their hands to cast spells," Ando explains. "But the Greys of Zamora focus on drawing sigils. So you can see the problem."

"No, I *can't*," you say. "How could a war be caused by something as simple as which of those two ways is right? That doesn't make sense!"

Ando shakes his head at your foolishness. "They're just too different. They use mutually exclusive types of magick!"

You shake your head. "This is the stupidest reason for a war that I've ever heard." Then you think of some of Earth's wars, and you wonder.

Turn to the next page.

Meanwhile, Trent walks over to the door. With a grunt, he pushes it open.

"Hey, it wasn't locked after all!" he says accusingly. "It's just heavy."

Damien shrugs. "I must have loosened it."

Ando looks you in the eye. "You are wise, so I will tell you the truth. It's possible that the Grey Council will suspect you are from the other side, and imprison you until after the war with the Blues is over. If you want to escape now, I know a way."

You grit your teeth. Escaping from a possibly dangerous situation sounds good. But your parents didn't raise you to run away from your problems.

If you decide to stay and speak to the Grey Council of Zamora, turn to page 61.

If you choose to escape the city with Ando, turn to page 131.

You, Trent, and Damien follow Faith down a path into the jungle. The other children follow behind.

You want to ask Faith a million questions, starting with how she knew Davy Cricket's name. But you can't stop staring at the jungle. The trees are seething with life and movement. You glimpse moving shapes in the shadows. Some of them are pretty big.

"Um, shouldn't you all be holding hands or something?" you suggest, and the kindergarteners quietly laugh at that as if that's the funniest thing they ever heard.

"It's a good thing I scared off those dinosaurs, anyway," says Damien.

Faith holds up her whistle. "Actually, they just hate dog whistles. All I have to do is blow on this and they run off."

"Dinosaurs are afraid of dog whistles?!" exclaims Trent. "That makes *us* the kings of the jungle."

You reach a clearing with a large firepit in the center. It's surrounded by massive trees. You notice they have strange scratch marks going about twenty feet up on their trunks. You also spot ladders built high into the trees, and you can see treehouse platforms far above.

"It's a tree city!" exclaims Damien.

Now the children cluster around you and start asking questions.

"How old are you?"

"Where are you from?"

"Can you do any magic tricks?"

Turn to page 56.

"Wait," you say. "First, I want you to tell *us* a story. Like, how did you get here?"

The kids all start talking at once, but you eventually learn they're in the same kindergarten class. Their teacher, Mrs. Edwards, was doing a lesson about local history. She took the class on a field trip to the oldest building near their school: the Time Travel Inn.

"When we got off the bus at the inn, nobody was around," says Faith. "But the door to one of the rooms was open, and Billy saw a triceratops inside. He screamed 'Dinosaur!' and all of us went in to see it. Then Jazmine found a machine and pushed some buttons on it."

"Sorry, *not sorry*," says a girl with a "Jazmine" name tag.

"That's how we got to the age of the dinosaurs. And luckily, Mrs. Edwards was transported with us. She taught us how to survive here."

Go on to the next page.

"Where is she now?" you ask, but Faith just looks away.

"What happened, Jurassic Dork?" Trent pulls the dog whistle from around Faith's neck. "What did you little monsters do to your teacher? Tell us!"

One little boy starts to cry, and then the rest of the children do, as you and Damien yell at Trent to stop it.

There's a loud *CRASH!* from the jungle, and everyone stops crying. The kindergarteners race for the tree ladders and climb to the tree houses. You stand listening to the crashes coming closer until Faith pulls you by the hand to a ladder and starts climbing.

As you and Damien scramble up behind her, a fearsome red dinosaur breaks into the clearing. It must be forty feet long, from the tip of its immense snout to the end of its tail.

"Oh wow, a *Tyrannotitan*," whispers Damien. "The tyrant titan!"

Turn to the next page.

You reach a treehouse platform and look down. Trent is still standing by the firepit! He looks scared, but defiant.

"I'm the new king of the jungle!" Trent shouts, and then he blows on the dog whistle. You can't hear the sound, but the tyrant titan can. The huge carnivore bellows and leaps forward, opening jaws with teeth like swords. This dinosaur isn't scared of the whistle!

Trent realizes his mistake and starts to run—but the dinosaur snaps him up in his jaws.

"*That's* what happened to Mrs. Edwards," whispers Faith.

Turn to page 60.

As the Tyrannotitan lumbers off into the jungle, something gleams on the platform and catches your eye. It looks like a mini version of the time machine back in Room 1!

"What's that?" you ask Faith.

"Mrs. Edwards took it off the desk at the Time Travel Inn," says Faith. "We don't know what it does."

"I think I do!" you say.

You grab the mini time machine and climb down the ladder. You see a digital readout with a number, and start spinning the dials and adjusting the settings. Davy Cricket jumps up on your shoulder as you gather the children together.

"Okay, is everyone here? I want you all to hold hands."

Faith looks at the time machine. "Wait, you're taking us back to normal time? But we don't want to go back!"

You are shocked. "Wait, you *knew* you could have gone back anytime? Why haven't you?"

"I know why," says Damien. "It's because this place has dinosaurs, right?"

The kids all nod. "It's awesome!"

You used to babysit in Florida, and letting these children stay here seems completely wrong. But Faith and her classmates are happier than any children you've ever known.

If you trick the children to go back to the present, turn to page 163.

If you decide not to make the kids leave this land, turn to page 177.

You look at Ando, not sure you can trust him.

"Take us to the Grey Council," you say.

Minutes later, he leads your group into the city's dome, where you gasp. You've never been in a space so huge! The domed space is so gigantic, it's like a special effect from a science fiction movie. You take a breath and catch up with your group. The four of you have to walk hundreds of yards to reach the group of twelve seated figures. There is also a large throne that nobody is sitting in.

"We are the Grey Council of Zamora," Lamonta says. "We have scant time to spend on these intruders, but we must decide what to do with them—"

"That girl," interrupts a wizened man on the left. "I know that face!"

You stand awkwardly as the other Council members lean forward to stare at you. "I'm sorry, sir, but that's not possible," you say. "I've never been here before in my life."

"I have it!" says the old man. "She looks like—"

His words are interrupted by a hurricane blast of wind from a window that scatters tables and tapestries. In through the window sails a flying carpet. Standing on top of it is a group of men and women dressed in blue. At the front of the group is a man with a fierce beard and a fiercer expression.

Turn to the next page.

"Is that a shag carpet?" asks Trent. "Because those are really hard to keep clean."

"Quiet, you fool," hisses Ando. "That's Ramsteen, the leader of the Blue Wizards!"

Ramsteen's voice is deep and powerful, even in the vast space of the dome. "Greetings, Grey Council of Zamora! Accept your loss and bow down before us Blue Wizards to avoid further bloodshed."

But the Grey Council members are already tracing the floor with their staffs, and above them the air grows thick with magick. You begin to understand why this dome is so huge. It has to be to contain the Grey Council's spells!

The Blue Wizards also act quickly. They form a circle and begin chanting and making elaborate hand gestures. From the space in their center, a massive bolt of blue energy rockets up and blows away the Greys' magick cloud as if it is nothing but smoke.

Turn to page 64.

Lamonta wilts. The other Council members also crumple to the floor. Ramsteen the Blue stands even straighter.

"With that loss, your magick wall outside will soon fail. Then the Blue army will pour into the city. And thanks to your stubbornness, there will be no way to stop their slaughter of your citizens."

"This is ridiculous!" you say. You think back to the conflict resolution plan your old school in Florida used. "Isn't there any way to stop this?" you whisper to Ando.

The boy shakes his head. "The only possibility would be if someone challenged Ramsteen to a duel and won. But that would be suicide."

You want to resolve this peacefully, because you're not an insane barbarian. But these Blue Wizards are blowing the joint up, and they only seem to understand force.

If you challenge Ramsteen to a duel, turn to page 79.

If you try to apply conflict resolution tools to the problem, turn to page 169.

You know you won't survive another battle in the Colosseum. As Spatula walks away, you call out, "Wait! What if I could share something more valuable than our fighting? It will make you rich beyond your dreams."

Spatula frowns. "Every gladiator promises outlandish things for their freedom. But you have already surprised me once today. So what is it?"

You think fast. What CAN you share with an ancient Roman that's worth something? You know about guns, printing presses, and solar power. But you don't completely understand how they work, and you can't actually *make* any of them.

"If you let me out, I'll prove I speak the truth."

Spatula reluctantly has a guard unlock the cell door. You are escorted through dark, torchlit halls to Spatula's office. His desk is covered with long sheets of papyrus that have messy columns of Roman numerals written on them.

Turn to the next page.

"I have a lot of accounting to do," says Spatula. "So speak quickly!"

You ask for papyrus and something to write with, and say, "I beg for one hour of your time. Then if you don't think what I have is useful, back to the arena I go."

Spatula leans forward. "Proceed."

Two hours later, Spatula leads you back to the gladiator cell. He unlocks the door and shouts, "Guards! Three cheers for our visitors!"

Cheering from the guards? you think. *That's a little surprising.*

Then the guards come forward with three *chairs*, and you realize you just heard wrong. As you, Trent, and Damien sit, Spatula gives a long prayer of thanks to Pluto, god of the dead, for sending him a math genius.

"What'd you do, Astrid?" whispers Trent.

Go on to the next page.

You grin. You tell the boys that when you saw the Roman numerals Spatula was using, you realized that you knew a better way. So you explained the Arabic number system of 1, 2, 3, 4, etc. By writing a Roman numeral next to each Arabic number (for example, "III = 3"), you showed Spatula how much easier it could be to add, subtract, multiply, and divide.

"Who knew math could save our lives?" asks Damien.

Spatula looks over. "You three are free to go and take up residence in my holiday home on the Via del Corso. Dentatus will accompany you as a bodyguard." Then a guard hands each of you a belt and wooden sword.

"A wooden sword? Is this a *joke*?" Trent demands.

Turn to the next page.

Dentatus quickly thanks Spatula and leads your group away.

"Your sword is a *rudis*," he explains. "Only retired gladiators wear them. The swords are a mark of honor, because the only way to get them is by killing a lot of people."

You emerge from the Colosseum's darkness into the light of Ancient Rome. Only nothing looks ancient! The streets and buildings are new. Curious Romans watch your group as you walk down the street. Most people are dressed in tunics and cloaks. Some notice your wooden sword and nod respectfully.

Then you see a strange, familiar figure waving to you from a stairway in a large opening in the street. It's the odd person you saw in Room XXXV of the Time Travel Inn! You recognize them by their many arms.

"Over there, quickly!" you tell Dentatus.

"Great Hades, into the *Cloaca Maxima*?" asks the gladiator. "The Great Sewer has access points from the streets, rivers, and the sea. Bandits lurk there, and giant octopi feed on humans! So I vote no."

"Why can't we just go to Spatula's vacation house?" Trent whines. He holds his wooden sword up by his face with a sour expression.

Relaxing in a villa sounds good after all you've been through. But you think the answers to why you came to Rome in the first place wait for you in the sewer.

If you insist on going down into the Great Sewer, turn to page 144.

If you continue on to Spatula's villa, turn to page 149.

The giant cricket cavorts in the snow. Your feet scrunch in the new powder as you slowly approach it.

"Easy, big fella," you say, holding your hands to your sides. "I just want to help."

The cricket freezes and cocks its head. It doesn't seem afraid as you get closer and reach out to it. Then a snowball hits the cricket. It makes a surprised "CHIRP" and leaps awkwardly away in the snow, heading up the covered walkway.

"Direct hit!" laughs Trent.

Furious with Trent, you chase after the cricket. More snow gusts under the walkway. You race toward the Time Travel Inn rooms that are farthest from the lobby: 32, 33, 34. You look around but can't see any sign of the giant cricket.

You decide you'll have to turn back and retrace your steps. Suddenly, there is a crashing sound from the room beside you. Its door sign is written in Roman numerals: XXXV. You take out the master key and use it. Opening the door, you start to step in even though the lights are off—but then you see movement inside. There is a person there in the shadows, and there is something odd about the way they move.

You freeze with indecision. Whoever or whatever is in front of you, they're vandalizing your family's property. Uncool! But Trent and Damien are still way back by the lobby, and something about this room gives you the creeps.

If you slam this door shut, turn to page 92.

If you yell and confront whatever's inside room XXXV, turn to page 139.

You look at the ragtag group of kindergarteners. If these kids can survive in prehistoric times, it obviously can't be *that* hard.

"Are you ready?" asks Faith.

You shake your head. "Thanks, but we're going to explore on our own for a while."

The kindergarteners gather around Faith for a meeting. The children are all armed—could they force you to come with them?

You're relieved when Faith says, "You're older than us, so you must know what you're doing. Be sure to keep your eyes on the skies!" The kindergarteners then troop up their trail and disappear.

The rest of the jungle looks impenetrable, so you lead the boys down the beach. Out in the open, you can see if there's any danger coming.

"We are going to be SO famous when people hear about this," says Trent.

"But what did Faith mean by 'Keep your eyes on the skies'?" asks Damien.

Trent shrugs. "It's just a saying, like, 'In a while, crocodile—'"

There is a beat of leathery wings, and a dark shadow glides across the sand. You look up as a massive pterodactyl squawks, swoops, and scoops Trent up in its beak.

Turn to the next page.

You and Damien scream and start to run after it, but it's hopeless. Trent is gone.

"At least now we know what 'Keep your eyes on the skies' means," Damien says, as the giant reptile flies off. "And we need to get off this beach *now*."

The two of you run toward the jungle and plunge into the heavy foliage. Soon, you are hopelessly lost. Frustrated and sad, you sit on a mammoth log. A massive white snake makes eye contact with you from its perch in a nearby tree.

"Damien, we're not going to survive like this," you say. "We have to find those kids again."

Damien rummages in his fanny pack and pulls out what looks like a remote control. It's made of chrome and crystal like the time machine. "I took this from Room 1," he says. "Should I try to use it?"

You just stare at him. "Duh! Why didn't you say you had it?"

Damien shrugs. "I was having fun until Trent got eaten." He makes a few adjustments on the remote control.

Go on to the next page.

The white snake unwraps itself from a branch and slithers down the tree.

"Hurry, Damien, *hurry*!" you implore. Incredibly, the huge snake is already upon you. It's pulling back its head to strike.

The jungle flickers and then disappears. In a flash, it's replaced by a snowy forest.

"*That* was a close call," you say. You and Damien walk around a little and see a road.

"I recognize this!" Damien tells you, and you both walk faster.

A half hour later, the two of you stumble back into the lobby of the Time Travel Inn. You both sit in chairs, exhausted and silent.

The television is still set on a history channel, and it's playing footage of a recent fossil discovery:

> ". . . now we have more news on an amazing find from a fossil dig in Wisconsin today. Paleontologists have confirmed that they have dug up the bones of a *human* child from the Mesozoic Period. That means these human bones date back hundreds of millions of years, when dinosaurs roamed the planet! The scientific community is in an uproar—"

"Wow," says Damien. "Well, Trent always did want to be famous!"

The End

You steel yourself for a battle. As you do, the giant smashes one of his two opponents in the side with his axe. The man collapses like a tree that's been cut down. Then the massive gladiator glances over at you.

"I'll have you infants for dessert!" he bellows.

"Weapons!" hisses Damien. "We need weapons!"

Knives and short swords litter the arena floor, but using these in a fight would bring you much too close to that deadly axe. Instead, you pick up a long spear and heft it high. Then you take two short steps and throw the spear at the giant. The spear wobbles a little but flies true.

But the giant easily dodges out of the way and laughs scornfully.

You spot a defeated gladiator with a trident and a net. You grab them both. Then you turn to Trent and Damien and give them some quick instructions. You hand Damien the net.

"Good luck," you tell the boys. "Don't let me down!" you finish, racing away.

The giant is raining blows down on the man with the eagle crest on his helmet, forcing him to the ground. So you approach from behind and jab the trident into the giant's hairy back. He howls, turns, and swings the axe at you—but you are already running. You hear heavy footsteps following as you run in a wide circle back to the eagle-helmet man.

Go on to the next page.

You stand over the man in the eagle helmet.

"Stay down," you gasp. "And act defeated. Then when I count to three, we attack him."

"It's our funeral," he says. "Mars, give us strength!"

Thinking you are tired, the giant walks up to you casually, waving at the crowd. They cheer. The giant swings his axe, and the blade whistles through the air. "Listen to that crowd!" he shouts. "They love me."

"One," you whisper. "Two . . ."

"I must take my time with you," says the giant. "After all, the people should get their money's worth."

"Three!" you say, leaping forward and thrusting the trident. The giant's mighty axe chops the trident's pole in half. At the same time, the man next to you jabs out with his sword. The giant smiles and turns gracefully to avoid the blade.

Since the giant's slightly off-balance now, you push your broken trident pole into his chest as hard as you can. This forces him to step back. And that's perfect, because Trent and Damien have crawled forward and stretched the dead gladiator's net tight behind the giant's legs.

Turn to the next page.

76

The massive warrior's eyes widen in surprise and his arms spin for balance. The giant falls! Then the man with the eagle helmet pounces. You turn away, but you hear awful crunches. The crowd goes berserk. You can't tell if they're happy or enraged.

You grab your grandmother's diary from the dirt just before Roman guards rush onto the arena floor. They escort you, Damien, Trent, and eagle-helmet in front of what looks like the VIP seating.

A man steps forward and the crowd quiets down. "Caesar compliments you on your victory, and looks forward to your next events!" he shouts.

Roman soldiers escort you and your companions through a gate with the words *Porta Triumphalis* on it.

From there, you are led onto a wooden platform that drops, elevator-style, below the arena floor. You walk past a complex system of cells. Inside, gladiators and even bears and lions are locked in.

People bustle everywhere; it's a little like going below the decks of a mighty ship, or being backstage at an immense play.

Your group is locked in a large cell with rusty bars. You sit on a stone floor. Trent is pale and exhausted, and even Damien is silent with his thoughts.

Turn to page 78.

Looking for answers, you open your grandmother's diary:

> "My calculations show a moment in the near future when, for some reason, time stops for the human race. I call it the Doomsday Event, and have traced its beginning to key moments in the past. My plan to stop this event involves traveling back—"

"I have questions!" interrupts Damien. He ticks them off on his fingers. "Is this a weird dream? What was that thing back in the motel room? Did we really just travel through time to Ancient Rome? And who is *this* guy?"

The gladiator laughs. "I am Dentatus. And Rome is not 'ancient'! It is young compared to Babylonia or Greece. But the Roman Empire *is* vast. What province do you three come from?"

Before you can try to explain Wisconsin to this gladiator, a smiling man approaches the bars.

"Bless you, young warriors! The gods favored me with your magical appearance today. I am Spatula, owner of all gladiators at the Colosseum. You did so well, I have scheduled you for another battle in two days. Now excuse me. I must add up my profits. Even using our advanced Roman math, it will take me all night." He begins to walk away.

These battles are to the death, and there's no way you'll get lucky and survive a second time. Maybe there's a way to talk Spatula out of this?

If you ask Spatula to wait, turn to page 65.

If you decide to wait and make a plan with your cellmates, turn to page 84.

You step forward. "I will do what it takes to resolve this without any death. I challenge you to a duel, Ramsteen."

Ramsteen laughs. "A duel with YOU as the Greys' champion? That will result in at least one death: yours."

You shrug. "I challenge you."

"To make it more even, let's include your magick-less friends on your side," says Ramsteen, and the Blue Wizards snicker.

Lamonta limps forward, supporting herself with her stick. "This is dangerous, Astrid, but I see you are intent on going through with it. You have great natural talent, so all I can do is wish you good luck."

You're not sure when the magick duel officially starts. *Does someone start a clock or something?* you wonder. You take your chalk and bend down, trying to imagine a spell that would drive the Blues from the city. Your hand scrawls sigils on the floor in front of you, and time slows down. You look up at Ramsteen. You can see the pulse of a vein in his neck.

But before you can finish your sigils, Ramsteen's fingers bend into unlikely shapes. The next thing you know, you're flying backward through the air. Yet somehow, you're able to make a cool little somersault as you land and spring right back to your feet.

Turn to the next page.

You need to concentrate on Ramsteen and surprise him with something he wouldn't expect. So you scrawl a quick series of shapes on the floor and mutter "*Eelecurb.*" Suddenly, power courses through you; it's like you have hot chocolate in your veins!

You run toward your opponent, windmilling your arms. Your arms and legs move faster than they ever could on Earth. You reach the stunned Ramsteen. The sound of your magick fists hitting him is like a hailstorm hitting a maple tree.

Ramsteen is so taken by surprise, he doesn't try to block your punches. Instead, he backs up while doing a new finger dance. Blue flames engulf his fists, and he launches a punch at you. You slip under it and hop behind him. As Ramsteen turns, you reach up to his face and . . . tweak his nose.

Ramsteen freezes and blinks. Is he paralyzed? Did you hit some kind of wizardic nerve center?

Then the wizard smiles and shows all his teeth.

"While I have enjoyed your performance, the time has come for you to go away." He whips his arms back and forth, faster and faster, and a mighty whirlwind of power begins forming above the wizard. Wind fills your ears, and you know in your heart that you don't have time to stop this attack.

Go on to the next page.

Luckily, you still have your friends to help. Damien takes off his deer jacket, revealing a huge camo fanny pack around his waist. He unzips it and pulls out two short sticks connected by a chain. It's a mini pair of *nunchucks*?

While Ramsteen gazes up in admiration at the hurricane of destruction he's about to unleash on you, Damien creeps up on him. The other Blue Wizards try to shout warnings, but nobody can hear anything because of the howling wind. Damien twirls the nunchucks around his back, and then swings them over his shoulder and right at Ramsteen's skull.

THWOCK.

Ramsteen falls to the ground like a piñata, and his hurricane of destruction vanishes.

Turn to the next page.

There is silence in the dome, and then Lamonta addresses the Blue Wizards: "Take your vanquished champion and leave." Muttering in displeasure, they roll Ramsteen to their carpet, and in a whisk, the disappointed wizards fly back out the window.

Meanwhile, the wizened man on the Grey Council is studying your face again. "Aha!" he cries. "I've got who this girl reminds me of. She's—"

"Astrid!" calls a familiar voice.

You spin around. "Mom?!"

Your mother is walking across the dome to you! You sprint to her and the two of you hug for what seems like forever.

"Mom, what are you doing here?" you finally ask. "And how does that wrinkly old man know you?"

"Hey!" protests the wizened man.

"Where to begin!" says your mother. "Twelve years ago, Grandmother Dolores was missing. Although I was pregnant at the time, I traveled to the Time Travel Inn to look for her. I ended up discovering the same Doggy Door you did and used it to travel here, to Bellaquom. Like you, I came to the Grey City of Zamora. And then I went into labor."

"Wait—that means I wasn't even born on Earth?!"

"And not just that," says Lamonta, walking to the empty throne. "You also have saved our city from destruction and its people from death and enslavement. By Zamora's laws, that means you are entitled to be our queen."

Your jaw drops. You can be the queen of a magical land, just like that? But what about your whole life on Earth up to this point?

"You don't have to accept," Mom whispers to you. "You can decide."

If you decide to stay in Bellaquom as Queen of Zamora, turn to page 41.

If you choose to return to Earth with Mom, go to page 138.

Spatula disappears into the dark hallways of the Colosseum. You hear him tell a guard to get "the strange youths" anything they need.

You turn to Damien and Trent. "Look, I don't know how, but we're in Ancient Rome, and they're going to make us fight again. We need a plan to survive *now*, before we can try to get back to the present."

"Sorry to butt in," says Dentatus, "but this IS the present."

Damien grins. "We're going to be fine! We just have to explain to the Romans about cell phones, dinosaurs, cars, atoms, and rockets, and they'll think we're geniuses."

Trent pulls out his cell phone. "Really? My phone doesn't even turn on anymore! It's just a chunk of metal and plastic. Besides, telling Romans about rockets or cars will just make them think we're crazy."

"*I* don't think you're crazy," Dentatus says.

You point to Damien's camouflage fanny pack. "But don't our clothes seem odd to you?"

Dentatus shrugs. "You're at the center of the mighty Roman Empire. We get all types here."

Go on to the next page.

You quiz Dentatus about the gladiators' weapons, and he explains there's an armory workshop where the weapons are made, repaired, and stored.

You call out to the guard and ask to visit the armory. To your surprise, the guard unlocks the cell and escorts you down long hallways to a large room lit with torches.

Spears, swords, and tridents are everywhere. A scarred man with one eye looks at you.

"Ah, the new girl," he says. "Spatula told me that you should get special treatment. I am Hannibal. What do you need?"

You ask Hannibal if he can work with wood. His eye lights up. He explains that he was an expert wood craftsman in North Africa before being captured by the Romans. Hannibal gets you papyrus, an inkpot, and a small, pointy piece of wood to draw with so you can show him what you want.

As you start sketching a diagram, Hannibal asks, "Is it a torture device?" You laugh and explain the kinds of wood, twine, and feathers that are needed. Hannibal then summons workers, and soon the sounds of sawing fill the air.

Turn to the next page.

Hours later, you return to your cell, exhausted. The boys pepper you with questions, but you ignore them. You fall asleep in the corner. When you wake up, you ask to be taken back to the armory.

"No way!" says Trent. He must be getting his courage back. "We need to come with you this time," he insists.

So all of you return to the armory together.

Hannibal seems to have worked all night. He proudly hands over a sample of your design.

"Hannibal, you are a genius!" you exclaim, passing the sample to Dentatus. The gladiator turns the strange object around in his hands.

"It this a torture device?" he asks.

"No," you answer. "It's a *crossbow*."

Turn to page 88.

A worker brings you one of the small arrows that you sketched the day before.

"See, you turn this crank back to pull the bowstring into place," you explain. "Then you load the arrow, it's called a bolt, here. Now, see here underneath? This is the trigger. Be careful not to push it—"

Damien reaches over and pushes the crossbow trigger. There is an immediate "twang," and the bolt is launched into the hallway. A moment later, you hear a cry of pain, and Spatula rushes in.

"Which of you fools just shot my cook in the leg?" he demands. Damien points at Dentatus, who points at Hannibal, who points at you. Spatula notices the crossbow.

"What is that, a new torture device?" he asks.

"I thought it was for torture too!" says Hannibal. As he explains the crossbow, you go check on the cook. It turns out the crossbow bolt caught him in the meaty part of his leg, so he should be all right.

Go on to the next page.

You make sure his wound is wrapped in bandages that have been boiled, which results in a long conversation. ("Why do we have to boil the bandages?" "To kill germs." "To kill what?" "Just do it!")

You return to the armory just as a sneezing man with a troop of bodyguards arrives.

"Hail Caesar!" cries Spatula. Everyone freezes and hails the sneezing Caesar.

"Spatula," sniffles the Roman emperor, "I wanted to speak to you about your new gladiators, but they are already here." He sneezes, then spots the crossbow. "Say, that looks like—"

"It's *not* a torture device," Trent interrupts.

"—a bow for small people," Caesar finishes, glaring at Trent.

Turn to page 91.

You explain the crossbow. Caesar then insists on a demonstration of it.

"I will need a target," says Caesar. "A human target." He points directly at Trent. "You, the boy who just interrupted me. You'll be perfect." Caesar sneezes again.

You protest, but you are not given any choice in the matter. Luckily Caesar tells you that he won't try it here. He will take all of you and the crossbow to his palace.

Before leaving, Caesar orders Hannibal to make more crossbows. Then you are taken to Caesar's palace, where you are surprised to see cats *everywhere*. "What can I say. I'm a cat person!" sneezes the Roman emperor.

You guess that he has an allergy, and suggest that the palace be carefully cleaned and the cats restricted to certain rooms. Your plan works! Caesar's sneezing immediately improves, and he considers you to be an invaluable wise woman. Dentatus is made the head of the Bureau of Barbarians, while Damien is happy to wander the palace and amuse people with his outlandish stories.

Caesar never forgives Trent for the interruption, but he does let him live.

You are kept under careful watch, and as the years pass, you wonder what became of your parents. Eventually, you think your memories of being from the future are all just some fantastic dream.

The End

You peer into the darkness for just a second longer and take a deep breath. Yes, there is definitely something wrong here—for one thing, the "person" you're seeing seems to have too many arms!

You step back and close the door.

"What's wrong now?" asks Damien as he jogs to reach you.

"I'm not sure, but we should definitely look somewhere else." You start walking back to the lobby.

Trent throws his arms up. "This is dumb! We're supposed to be looking for your parents, but you don't want to actually *look* anywhere."

You slow down as you walk by Room 32 again. Its sign catches your eye as you pass. The sign for Room 32 is tiny compared to the others. Maybe it's a clue.

"I'll look in here," you tell Trent. "Come on."

Go on to the next page.

You unlock the door and you all step inside. The wind gusts the door shut behind you and Damien jumps a little, but the room looks completely normal.

The only odd thing is a laptop-sized device made of chrome and crystal on a desk. It has a small stamp on the side reading "Short-Jump Device for Quick Fixes."

There is a knock at the door.

"Did someone call room service?" asks Damien.

"More like *doom* service," complains Trent.

You know that if the person outside was Mom or Dad, they'd come in, because they own the motel. So who is it? You're done running away from mysteries, so you open the door.

Turn to the next page.

A girl is standing there, but you're confused. You know her face from *somewhere*. For a moment, you wonder, *Is she someone famous?* Then you realize the truth and stagger back a step.

"Hi," the girl says. "Surprised?"

"Hey," says Trent, looking over your shoulder. "Why didn't you tell us you have an identical twin, Astrid?"

Because the girl IS you. You look *exactly* the same—the same almond-colored eyes, the same curly hair. And, even weirder, this Astrid is dressed identically to the way you are now.

Astrid II doesn't come inside. "Hey guys, can I talk to my sister alone?" she asks nervously.

Trent and Damien look a little offended. They back away and start poking around the hotel room. Then Astrid II whispers, "I don't have time to explain, but I'm *future* you. Now leave that device on the desk alone and get out of this room right now!"

Turn to page 96.

Astrid II looks over her shoulder. "I have to go, but remember what I said." And then she winks and runs off.

"Hey Astrid, what's your sister's name?" asks Damien.

"And why is she so weird and bossy?" demands Trent. "Kind of *dumb* how you guys dress exactly the same. Do your *parents* make you do that?!"

"Quiet, Trent!" you say. He may be your new friend, but you're already pretty sick of his teasing.

You need to think. On the one hand, it seems to be *you* who told you to leave this room now.

But on the other hand, if that WAS you from the future, Astrid II would know that you hate being told what to do. And why wouldn't Astrid II give you a reason why?

You sit in a chair. "You guys, I don't have a sister. That girl said she was me from the future, Astrid II. And Astrid II told me to leave this room."

"Okay, then let's go," says Damien.

"But she might have been using reverse psychology, because Astrid II would know that I hate being told to do something without a reason. Plus, why did Astrid II give me that weird wink? I'm not a winker!"

"So you're saying we should *stay* in the room?" asks Damien.

You press your palms to your forehead so that you can think.

If you follow Astrid II's advice and leave, turn to page 101.

If you decide Astrid II actually wanted you to stay put, turn to page 117.

You leap into the toy plane's cockpit while the Jabberwock batters the door from the other side. Its blows leave bulging dents in the steel. Searching frantically, you find a small half-sphere of glass under the dashboard, with a label: "In case of emergency, break glass."

There's a loud *smash* as the entire doorframe splinters, and the steel door tilts inward. So you punch and break the glass, cutting your knuckles. You reach inside and pull out a tiny remote control. It has a red button and a small dial like the one on the dashboard.

"Hurry!" screams Trent.

Turn to page 99.

A massive head on a long neck peeks through the bent steel doorway. You frantically set the remote's dial to "Earth-1" and push the button as the huge head snakes toward you—

And then you're back in the basement at the Time Travel Inn!

I'm home again, you think. The three of you sit there for a moment in silent shock.

Turn to the next page.

"We made it," says Trent quietly. "Somehow, mostly thanks to me, we survived."

"Sorry about the whole kazoo-Jabberwock thing," says Damien.

The three of you go upstairs. As you close the trapdoor leading to the Doggy Door, you hear familiar voices out in the lobby.

"Mom? Dad?" You race out and see your parents surveying the hole in the wall that Redclaw made.

"Oh, Astrid, we were worried sick about you!" Mom says. "Are you okay?"

"I'm fine, but where were YOU?" you demand. "We've been looking everywhere!"

Your parents exchange a look.

"Honey, I was just looking for Grandmother Dolores, but I didn't find her," says Mom. "But you're here now, that's the most important thing. And who are these two young gentlemen?"

You introduce the two boys. Then Damien checks his watch. "Oops, I have to go. Want to come over for dinner, Astrid? We're having lasagna."

You look at the giant hole in the wall and at how your parents are acting as if everything's normal. "No thanks," you say. "I have some questions for these two that can't wait."

The End

You just warned yourself to get out of this room! Since it's hard to think of anyone you trust more than *you*, you decide to leave.

"Come on," you tell the boys. "The search for my parents continues."

Trent mutters, "This is getting us nowhere." But as the three of you trudge down the walkway, you notice something odd. The rooms are numbered 31, 30, 92, and 28. You backtrack to Room 92.

"Hey, that's '29' backward!" you say. You open Grandmother Dolores's diary and hand Damien the master key. "Open it up while I check to see if my grandmother wrote anything about this."

Damien uses the key, swinging the door open into a bathroom. "How weird!" he exclaims. "Good thing someone wasn't in here." The three of you walk in and see that the bathroom opens up to a motel room with a familiar chrome-and-crystal device on a nightstand.

"So this room's design is backward, too," says Trent, walking over to the device.

Turn to the next page.

"Uh-oh," you say. "Grandmother's notes say this room is an experiment in *reverse* time. She says it's still in progress, and we should be careful not to turn on that device's power button."

Trent walks to the chrome-and-crystal machine. "Turn on its power, got it."

"No!" you cry, but it's too late, because Trent pushes the button the pushes Trent because, late too it's but, cry you "No!"

"It got, power its on turn." Machine crystal-and-chrome the to walks Trent.

"Button power device's that on turn to not careful be should we and, progress in still it's says she. Time reverse in experiment an is room this say notes Grandmother's." Say you, "Oh-uh."

The End

"Over here!" you yell out. "Help!"

The footsteps stop, then shuffle toward you from behind. You can't turn to see whoever is behind you, but their shadow is visible. It seems much larger than it should be.

A hearty chuckle makes the air vibrate, and a woman's deep voice says, "Ah, three young frozen humans. It's my lucky day." There is a sniffing sound. "From the smell of this magick, you were spell-bound by a mere child? For shame."

To your side, you see Damien being plucked off the ground and into the air, then Trent. It happens so fast, the boys barely have time to yelp. Then your visitor comes around in front of you. She stands about fifteen feet tall. She carries a coarse bag holding Trent and Damien.

"A most excellent haul," says the giantess. "I will sell these two as workers, but YOU, my dear, are special. Magick radiates from you as if you were a warm ember. I know a wizard who'd pay a pretty sack of gold for you."

"But I don't want to be a wizard's apprentice," you say.

The giantess laughs. "You won't be one, my dear. Instead, you'll likely be locked in a dungeon somewhere and used as a, um, magical source of power like a, um, what's the word . . ."

"Like a battery?" volunteers Damien from inside the bag.

"Yes!" agrees the woman. "Like a magical battery."

The giantess picks you up easily and clasps you under her arm. As she strides through the forest, you wonder what would have happened if you'd stayed quiet—and what your new life as a magical battery will be like.

The End

You walk to the bottom of the stairs and call up, "Who's there?"

A woman and a man wearing tight red coveralls race down the stairs. "Freeze!" the woman shouts. "You're all under arrest."

"What?" you demand. "Who are you? What are you doing down here? This is private property!"

The man pulls out a gleaming badge.

"We're Multiverse Police, and you're about to be in violation of Bylaw 57.1, Appendix B: Unauthorized Multiverse Jumping. It's a serious crime."

"The only crime here is your leotards," scoffs Trent.

The male agent blushes. "They're *unitards*." He walks over to the plane and grabs its instruction manual. "And this contraband is ours. Now come with us, because—"

"Hold on." The woman presses a hand to her ear. "We've got an emergency in Sector 97?" She looks at you. "This is your lucky day, so we're letting you children off with just a warning. Now if you want to avoid an untimely death, get out of this basement and forget you ever saw it."

And with that, she and the man sprint up the stairs and are gone.

Turn to page 106.

“Well, that was unexpected,” says Damien.

“Yeah, I just got *unexpectedly* robbed in my own house!” you exclaim. “I don’t know who those clowns think they are, but they’re not getting away with this.”

Trent grins. “Yeah, I can just hear that phone conversation. ‘Hello, police? Two strangers in leotards stole my grandma’s multiverse diary.’”

“*Unitards*,” you correct, getting back in the plane’s cockpit. “And I don’t need to call the police, because I can take care of this myself. Now get in if you’re coming.”

Go on to the next page.

Damien and Trent shrug and climb aboard. The dashboard's dial is set to "Earth-1." You click it forward to a choice that reads "Mythtaken." Damien pops his two quarters into the coin slot. As the quarters rattle down, the plane jolts into motion, lurching forward and rolling back, only to lurch forward again.

"Some ride," mocks Trent . . .

And in a blink, the three of you are at the end of a wide hallway! A woman sitting at a desk looks up. "Oh, hello!" she says. "I didn't think we had anyone from your area scheduled for today. And my, your group is young *and* unarmed? You must be extremely gifted."

Turn to the next page.

You're tongue-tied, but Trent plays it cool. "We are extremely gifted. But, um, where ARE we?"

The woman stands up. "Satyrus, of course." As she walks out from behind the desk, you gasp. She has the legs of a deer! Seeing you stare, the woman says, "Oh, I forget that you humans are so sheltered. You've heard of fauns, correct? Half-human, half-goat, from Greek mythology?"

She doesn't wait for an answer. Instead, the faun walks briskly to a massive steel door. "You'll want to get started right away. But just a reminder before you begin: Whatever you do, don't disturb the Jabberwock."

"'Get started'?" you repeat, feeling lost. "'The Jabberwock'?"

The faun frowns and points to a sign on the wall.

NOTICE:
1. Griffins' tears work wonders
2. Beware the Jabberwock!

"As you know, a griffin's tear is powerful magic. It can even bring the dead back to life."

"That sounds fake," Trent says.

"Yeah, are you sure you're not thinking of phoenixes?" you offer.

"Is that still what they're teaching you?" the faun asks, rolling her eyes. "And as for the Jabberwock," she continues, "the less said, the better." She throws an immense bolt off the steel door and pushes the door outward while impatiently motioning you through the doorway. "Well, what are you waiting for?"

"Um," you cleverly reply.

If you follow the faun's orders, turn to page 110.

If you stay to ask more questions, turn to page 128.

110

The faun waves the three of you out the mammoth door. "Good luck on your hunt. When you're done, just knock three times on this door." Then the massive door slams shut in your face, and you find yourself outdoors. The door itself is set in a steep hillside. It overlooks a meadow, and beyond that is a forest.

"This is all so WEIRD!" exclaims Damien. "But if we're on a hunt, it's a good thing I brought weapons." He rummages in a camo fanny pack and pulls out a ridiculously small pair of nunchucks. "Stay behind me if anything gets scary," he says, twirling them around.

Trent just rolls his eyes. "Anyway, how're we going to find your parents and grandmother, Astrid?"

"Let's ask them," you say, just as a group of small people emerge from the forest. Its members are heavily armed, with spears, rifles, and even what looks like a bazooka. "Wait, are those . . . *leprechauns*?"

Suddenly, there is a chilling roar from above, and a mammoth winged lion with an eagle's head swoops down from the sky. It lands in the center of the group, pouncing on an unlucky leprechaun. The rest of the group start screaming and running away.

Go on to the next page.

"That's a griffin!" Trent exclaims. The leprechauns have all scattered, so you and the boys try to quietly tiptoe away.

"Hello!" the griffin calls out. It flaps its wings once and lands near you, the dead leprechaun in its talons. "Where are you three going?"

"Oh, hi!" you say. "We, uh, didn't see you there." The griffin's massive eagle head looks strangely familiar. Then Damien starts whipping his nunchucks around, so you add, "Don't worry! He's not dangerous, except to himself."

"Not dangerous?" The griffin chuckles. "Not dangerous!" It keeps laughing and gets so hysterical, a tear forms in one of its eyes and drops into the grass. "I am Murkwing," the griffin says after it catches its breath. "Few things on Satyrus are more dangerous than ME. So for the gift of laughter, I will spare your lives."

"Um, thank you?" you gulp.

"Just one more thing," says the griffin. "My brother, Redclaw, was kidnapped by a sorcerer named Dolores Alcindor. Do you know anything about it?"

"Oh!" You think about the huge eagle's head you saw in the Time Travel Inn's lobby. That must be Redclaw! You gulp, because Murkwing is watching you carefully.

If you deny knowing anything, turn to page 122.

If you tell Murkwing the truth about what you know, turn to page 134.

Grandmother Dolores warned you about this evil genius, so you swing your cutlass at his head. But the pirate captain blocks the blow, and then, with a flick of his wrist, he somehow pops the cutlass out of your hand.

"You lose!" he says. You spot a jar of ink on his desk. You whip the jar in his direction. Ink sprays across the pirate's face, blinding him. He staggers backward just as the ship rocks to the side, and his head hits the wall with a loud *thwock*.

The captain slides down to the floor, unconscious.

"Hurray!" you say aloud, just as the door opens. Four armed pirates escort Grandmother inside. The shortest of them is carrying Davy Cricket in a small cage, and that pirate sees the captain lying facedown.

"Murder!" he cries. "Murder most foul! We must keelhaul these stowaways!"

The pirates haul you, Davy, and Grandmother onto the deck above. Then the crew clusters around and has a long debate about whether they should flog, maroon, or keelhaul you.

Go on to the next page.

“Captain Einstein would want them to walk the plank,” says an immense pirate who must be the leader. The others grumble because apparently walking the plank is not really a pirate tradition, but they go along with it.

“But can we keep the cricket?” asks the short pirate. “It seems heartless to send it to Davy Jones’s locker.”

The other pirates discuss and agree to take a vote. It’s close, but they decide you all must go. Minutes later, you, Davy Cricket, and Grandmother Dolores are forced onto a long plank sticking out of the side of the ship.

Grandmother looks at you and says, “I hope you can swim.” She dives gracefully off. Davy then jumps after her, but you hesitate. The ocean is a long way down! The short pirate brandishes a long harpoon. “Don’t make me use this, Miss.”

“Okay, okay, I’m going,” you reply. As you look at his weathered features, you realize you have no idea of his age. “How old are you?”

“Me? I’m fifteen years old,” he replies.

You are shocked. “Has your life been especially hard?”

“Oh, no, Miss, just the usual: war, famine, starvation, and pestilence. How old are you?”

“I’m close to your age,” you say quietly.

Turn to page 115.

The boy-pirate laughs. “I thought you were younger, because you lack scars. Now forgive me, Miss, but off you go.” He pushes you with the wooden end of the harpoon. You plummet off the plank and splash awkwardly into the sea.

As you swim to the surface and spit out a mouthful of salt water, a man with a bandaged head rushes to the ship’s railing. “Sorry about all this!” he calls down in a German accent. “I wanted to talk to you, but too late now. It’s a bit hard to turn these ships around, you see. Best of luck!” The ship sails out of earshot.

“Um, you still have your time travel machine, right?” you ask.

Grandmother grimaces. “It fell out of my pocket and sank. So I think it’s time to impress me with your swimming, Astrid.”

From a perch on top of Grandmother’s head, Davy Cricket basks in the sun as Grandmother sets a strong stroke for what you hope is land.

The End

"Run!" you scream at Trent.

He sprints through the shallow water. Just when it looks like he's made it, the plesiosaur lurches through the surf like a gigantic seal from a nightmare. The dinosaur's neck stretches toward Trent, getting closer, closer . . . then its mammoth jaws *SNAP!* on Trent's hoodie, and it pulls him back down.

Moments later, the plesiosaur and Trent have vanished beneath the waves.

You and Damien collapse onto the sand and lie there, panting.

"Sorry about your friend," you say, meaning it. "I can't believe that just happened. Or DID it happen?" You whistle in disbelief. "And why'd we go back millions of years in time and land in water?"

Damien seems like he's in shock, but he says, "This part of Wisconsin was underwater way back then."

Despite the heat, you shiver. "But way back then is NOW."

Then you hear a deep hiss behind you. You spin around in time to see an absolutely terrifying red dinosaur charging at you. As its jaws open, you just have time to think that you've never seen such gigantic teeth.

The End

"That *had* to be reverse psychology," you decide, getting up. You walk to the room's device and see that it has a Power button. You turn that on, and a screen lights up reading: "EXECUTE 30 MINUTE JUMP?"

Damien and Trent exchange a look. "Wait," says Damien, "if this is a Chronometer Reversal Device, does that mean we're going 30 minutes back in time?"

"*If* it works," you say. "And if it does, then we can follow my dad and find out where he goes. You guys okay with that?"

"Sure," says Trent. "If I'm late getting home, I can always use that thing to go back in time half an hour."

You tap the device's screen, and the room pulsates for a moment.

"Hey," says Damien, looking out the window. "There's less snow out there!"

The three of you go to the door and open it. Outside, two boys are playing basketball in the parking lot. As they shoot, a moving truck pulls up in the driveway.

"Oh my gosh," says Damien. "That's ME out there! Why didn't anyone tell me how great I look?"

"Shh!" you say. "We can't attract attention to ourselves. Come on, let's hide outside."

Turn to the next page.

118

The three of you crouch low and scoot down the outer walkway. You hide behind a long planter. You watch the van park, then see Dad get out. He greets the boys, then walks past your hiding spot toward the back of the motel. You want to call out, but don't want to give Dad a heart attack since he just left you in the van.

So you let Dad pass by, then watch yourself get out of the van. "I'm Astrid," you hear yourself say to the boys, and then watch as you steal the basketball from Trent and dunk it.

"That was a foul," says the Trent next to you. You gesture for the boys to quietly follow you so that you can find out where your father went. But as the three of you turn the corner after him, a girl stops you.

"What are you doing here?!" Astrid II demands. "I specifically told you to get out of that room!"

"I know," you say. "But I thought you knew that I *wouldn't* do it unless you specifically told me *why* I should. Plus, you winked, and I thought that meant you were kidding."

Go on to the next page.

"I don't know why I did that," grimaces Astrid II. "I was just freaking out about meeting myself, and I panicked!"

"This is the worst time-management problem in history," you say. "How do we solve it?"

Astrid II holds up your grandmother's journal. "Grandmother Dolores discovered that you can travel back in time to *before* you were born and return without a problem. But if you only go a short distance back, it creates issues. Like a double you. Me. Whoever."

"Triple you, now," says Damien. "And double us." His eyes are getting glazed over as he watches himself playing basketball.

"You only traveled back in time a half hour. Plus, you arrived at the same location you already were." Astrid II opens the diary and reads aloud: "This creates a 'closed self-consistency time loop.' The key is not to START a loop, because then events are caught in a cycle."

You think for a moment. "But why don't I just sneak into Room 32 and use the machine to stop me from time-traveling a half hour back in the past in the first place?"

Astrid II gives you a look. "Duh. I already tried that. How do you think I got here? Look, it's happening now!" You look down the walkway to Room 32 and see Astrid II (or III?) knock on the door. The door opens, and she talks to the Astrid (you?) in the room.

Turn to the next page.

120

Astrid II sighs. "That's ME, and look where it got us. Based on Grandma's diary, any actions taken by us now have existed all along. The future, past, and present are all stuck in the same loop." She looks over your shoulder. "And look, the party just keeps getting bigger."

The door to Room 32 opens, and out come Damien, Trent, and *you*. You start to panic, realizing there are at least four Astrids at the Time Travel Inn now.

"But how do we fix this?" you ask in desperation.

An angry voice startles you. "ASTRID! I am so mad at us!" You turn and see *another* you. "Why couldn't you follow our own directions?!"

The door to Room 32 opens again, and you can hear Astrids and Damiens and Trents meeting each other. The Damiens start picking teams for a basketball game, but two of the Trents start fighting each other.

What a mess! You are really, really starting to wish that you had listened to yourself.

The End

"Come on!" you cry to the boys, racing after the faun. She sees you following and waves you down a side corridor.

"You can't keep up with me," she says, "and the Jabberwock will catch you in a moment." She points to a tiny wooden door set in the wall. "This is a secret route back to safety. Now take it, and close the door behind you!" And with that, she dashes off and is gone.

You kneel down and open the door. On the other side is a snow drift. Behind you, the horrible burbling sound of the Jabberwock grows closer.

"Here goes nothing," you say, and plunge into the snow. Shivering, you stand up and help the boys crawl through. Then you slam the little door shut and look around.

"Hey, we're back home!" says Damien, pointing to the sign for the Time Travel Inn.

You feel a vast sense of relief as you run into the inn's lobby. As you blow on your hands to warm up, Trent asks, "*Where* exactly did the faun say the little door went to?"

"She said 'safety.' Why?"

Trent just points. Outside the window, a herd of animals are walking through the parking lot.

They're unicorns.

The End

Damien starts to say something, but you elbow him and say, "We don't know anything! If we hear anything, we'll tell you immediately." The griffin nods, spreads its wings, and flies off, with the deceased leprechaun still in its talons.

"But Astrid, that griffin thinks your grandma's a wizard!" says Damien.

"Yeah, but let's not let the griffin know what WE know just yet," you say.

Meanwhile, Trent is looking in the grass where the griffin was.

"Help me look!" he yells to you. You and Damien join him in the grass.

"For what?" you ask Trent.

Go on to the next page.

"'Griffins' tears work wonders,' remember?" says Trent. "Find the teardrop!" Sure enough, he finds the griffin's tear. It's hardened into what looks and feels like transparent rubber.

Trent puts it in his pocket, and the three of you explore. You find the nearby ruins of what sort of looks like an ancient Greek temple built by giants. You also discover lots of skeletons, both human and fantastic. Their bones all have crushed skulls, missing limbs, and other marks of violence. You look for any signs of your parents or grandmother, but you don't dare do something as risky as calling out for fear that you'll attract unwanted attention.

The three of you enter the shadowy outskirts of the woods. As you do, you hear a voice call out, "Hello, kin of Alcindor."

Turn to the next page.

A centaur stands before you. He has chestnut-brown fur on his horse half. On his human half, he has a vibrant gray beard and is wearing a "University of Wisconsin" hoodie.

"How did you know I'm an Alcindor?" you ask.

The centaur sniffed. "I can smell it. I'm Pholóēs, by the way. How is your grandmother?"

"I don't know. I was hoping to find her here."

The centaur shakes his head. "It's been years since I've seen Dolores, and you're the first relative of hers I've met. I was the first to greet your grandmother when she arrived here at Satyrus," he says with pride.

"And did you . . . *eat* my grandmother?" you ask the centaur nervously.

"Certainly not!" says the centaur, offended. "The two of us made an arrangement. She would charge hunters from other worlds to come here and hunt for trophies. She used their money to pay for her scientific experiments."

"But what did *you* get out of the deal?" you ask, still suspicious.

"Friendship!" Pholóēs spreads his arms wide: "We all did. Look." You see a number of sprites and wood-like elves peeking shyly at you from around tree trunks and branches.

Turn to page 126.

UNIVERSITY OF
WISCONSIN

"Satyrus is home to many gentle folk," says the centaur. "These woods alone have dryads, kobolds, fairies, and platypuses."

"Platypuses? Funny," says Trent sarcastically.

"What's so funny about it?" a voice quacks from the stream. You look, and sure enough, it's a talking platypus.

Pholóēs explains that the new off-world hunters go after the predators who would otherwise harm his gentler friends.

"But two griffins objected to your grandmother's arrangement," Pholóēs continues. "So together, we *removed* one of them from the equation. By the way, does Dolores know you're here?"

"Nobody does," you say. "And we really must be going."

"I'm afraid not," says Pholóēs. "You know too much now, so I'm afraid you must stay. But don't worry! You and your companions will make fine homes for the birds. In time, you will be dryads yourselves."

Go on to the next page.

The centaur is clearly insane! You try to run away, but your feet are rooted in place. Looking down, you see that your legs are now wooden trunks. You look over at Trent, and his face is already puckered into a wooden grimace.

"Astrid?" says Damien as his hair turns to leaves. "I'm not going to make it home in time for dinner, am I? It was LASAGN----" Damien's last word is cut off as bark covers his mouth.

You try to reach into your pocket to get the griffin's tear, but your arm won't cooperate. Holding your hand in front of your face, you see bark form over your fingers.

Then a wren flies down and lands on it.

You are a tree.

The End

128

"Would you mind if we stayed inside here for a little while?" you ask.

The faun shakes her head. "You paid a lot of money to go hunting here, but if you insist. Maybe you'd like to see the Hall of Trophies first?" She gestures down the hall. You can see there are large objects mounted on the walls, but can't make them out. Walking closer, you see they are—

"What the heck?" demands Damien. "These are all monster heads!"

He's not wrong. There is a huge head near you of what looks like an immense fanged armadillo. Next to it is a woman's head, but she has both antennae and antlers. There are familiar heads from myths and folklore. You see the nine serpentine heads of a hydra, and right next to it is a golden retriever! And down the hall, you can see a red dragon head the size of an electric car protruding from the wall.

"Cool!" says Trent. "People pay to travel to Satyrus to hunt. Then they mount their trophies here!"

"But people aren't the only ones who hunt here," you say. "Look!"

Turn to page 130.

130

Someone new has materialized on your airplane. It looks like a tall baboon covered in scales, and it's wearing a gown that shimmers and reflects the light. The creature speaks quietly to the faun, and you hear her answer: "Yes, those three are fair game. But be careful—based on their harmless appearance, they must be quite dangerous indeed."

"You guys!" you whisper to the boys. "We have to get out of here—"

But even as you speak, a dart suddenly appears in Damien's neck. His eyes go wide, and he collapses. Trent topples next, and then you feel a sting in your arm. Your knees turn to water, and as you fall, you see the scaly baboon towering over you. It pulls out a large knife.

Luckily, the dart must have paralyzed your nervous system, so you barely feel it as your head is delicately and almost politely removed from your neck.

The End

You look at Ando carefully. You think an escape is the best choice. Can you trust him to get you out of here?

"Let's escape!" says Trent. "I don't want to be thrown behind bars here."

"I agree." Damien checks his watch. "I've got to be home in time for dinner tonight. We're having lasagna."

"We'll go with you," you tell Ando.

"The votes are in," says Ando. He holds a finger to his lips for silence, walks over to a bookcase, and taps on a panel. The bookcase slides into the wall, revealing a tunnel. The four of you enter, then Ando's staff lights up. The bookcase closes behind you.

For what seems like ages, you travel through closed-off hallways and tunnels and stairways. At one point, Ando opens a door and waves you toward it. You look through the doorway and see a vast warehouse filled with giant metal barrels. The air thrums with power.

"This is where Zamora stores the magick that powers the city's wall," says Ando. "We have to turn the wall off to escape." He points to a guard about fifty yards away. "Can you draw a sigil that knocks him out?" Ando asks you.

Turn to the next page.

132

You shrug. "I can try." You kneel down and start drawing shapes and numbers with chalk from the library. Words that almost make sense to you come to your lips as you focus on the idea of the guard falling unconscious. You draw a final circle and look up. The guard staggers a little and falls over.

"Wow, it's like magic!" you say, then realize how silly that sounds. Meanwhile, Ando has rushed forward and is doing something to the closest barrels. Suddenly, the thrumming sound stops and the warehouse is eerily quiet.

"Come on," Ando says. "Now we run for it!"

The four of you sprint out of the warehouse and find the city in chaos. "The city's walls have fallen!" people cry. Warriors dressed in blue attack the crowd. You dodge the fighting and focus on following Ando beyond where the city's invisible wall once stood. A group of twelve people in blue robes step out from the surrounding woods and approach you.

"I am Ramsteen, leader of the Blue Wizards," says a bearded man at the front. "I want to thank you for lowering Zamora's defenses. Our army is taking over the city and putting it to the torch."

Go on to the next page.

"I didn't mean to do that!" you protest.

"But I did," says Ando with a bow. "Thank you for the opportunity, master. These fools never suspected I was a Blue spy all along."

Ramsteen laughs and then looks carefully at Trent and Damien. Seeing they have no magical ability, he turns them into racoons that run off into the woods. Meanwhile, soldiers handcuff your hands behind your back.

"We will find a use for you in our new Blue Empire, child," says Ramsteen, as you watch Zamora go up in flames.

The End

134

You swallow hard, take a deep breath, and tell the griffin your entire story, ending with your arrival on Satyrus. You even describe the eagle head back at the inn.

After you finish, Murkwing nods. "I met your grandmother, Dolores, when she first linked Earth to Satyrus. She nicknamed our world 'Mythtaken,' which must be an example of human humor. Dolores proposed bringing hunters from other worlds to Satyrus to hunt for trophies. Naturally, my brother and I opposed it. So now I know how Redclaw was punished for this."

As the griffin speaks, you notice Murkwing's large teardrop in the grass at your feet. You pick it up; it feels like soft plastic. "Take that with you back to Earth and get Redclaw," the griffin says. "Your two friends will stay here with me."

"As hostages?" you ask.

"As guests. I'll even share my lunch with them." The griffin takes a bloody bite of leprechaun.

"Thanks, I'm good," says Damien.

Since you have no choice, you go to the steel door and knock three times. The faun lets you in and you take a seat in the airplane's cockpit.

Go on to the next page.

"Sorry, do you have any quarters?" you ask, and the faun reluctantly gives you a handful of random change. It includes steel washers, gold doubloons, and four quarters. You pop two into the coin slot . . .

And in a blink, you're back in the Time Travel Inn's basement! You hurry up to the lobby, where the giant eagle head is mounted on the wall. You'd thought its eyes were following you, but now you see they actually ARE. And now you know it *isn't* an eagle, it's an enchanted griffin!

"Hi, Redclaw," you say awkwardly. "Your brother Murkwing told me to put this in your beak. So please don't bite my hand off, and then I'll take you back to Satyrus."

Redclaw's head gives you the eagle-eye as you put the griffin tear in its mouth. Then the head blinks. "Oh, that's much better," says the griffin. "Now back up a little."

You do, and there is a terribly loud crash of splintered wood—the entire griffin has just stepped through the wall!

After shaking like a wet dog, Redclaw says, "I was trapped under a spell cast by an evil centaur. Now, shall we?"

Turn to the next page.

136

The two of you take the kiddie plane back to Satyrus. There, the two griffins greet each other warmly. Meanwhile, Trent and Damien have met a newly arrived trophy hunter named Nanoc, from another world in the multiverse. She is a blue-skinned warrior with a mammoth sword. And Nanoc is fascinated by Damien's fanny pack.

Murkwing approaches you. "Good news, Astrid. Redclaw is so happy to be home, he's agreed not to kill you and your friends."

"That *is* good news!" you say. But Murkwing isn't finished.

"Your portal between our worlds will stay open, but with just one small change. Instead of hunters coming to Satyrus, *we* will now start sending hunters to your Earth. True, humans are easy prey, but they are also delicious—wait, what is THAT doing here?" The alarmed griffin is pointing at Damien, who has pulled a random item from his fanny pack.

"It's a kazoo," you say.

"Don't let him blow it!" cries Murkwing. "A kazoo will disturb—"

Zweeoobbrrrrrrt!

Damien plays the kazoo loudly.

"— the Jabberwock!" finishes Murkwing. In a flash, the two griffins fly off together, and moments later, you hear a loud sound from the forest. You hear something BIG approaching, and it seems to be burbling as it comes.

Turn to page 31.

You look around at the dome and the wizards and your mother. Your head is spinning, so you take a deep breath and try to get your bearings.

"We can go home right now, just like that?" you ask.

"Just like that," Mom says. "We can get back to normal."

You start laughing. "'Normal'? In the last few minutes, I was in a magical duel with an evil wizard, found my mother, learned I wasn't born on Earth, and was just told that I can be the Queen of Zamora!"

You keep laughing until Damien softly asks, "Astrid? Are you okay?"

You stand up straight, as befits a queen. "I'm fine," you say. "Mom, let's go home." But in your heart, you know that you won't be getting back to normal anytime soon—if ever.

The End

The room is dim with dark shadows. You can make out the figure of someone in front of a desk, swinging a hammer to break something into pieces. There is something odd about the person's outline, almost as if they have too many arms.

You clench your grandmother's leather diary in case you need to use it as a weapon. You should yell at the intruder, but what? You have no idea who or what your adversary is, and they look possibly violent.

"Excuse me?!" you yell. "Um, this is my parents' inn and I can't find them right now but—"

The figure spins around. "Oh no!" it cries in a voice that sounds like popcorn popping.

Trent and Damien rush into the room to join you. As they do, the dimly lit figure pulls out a small gleaming device, and the next thing you know, *everything* *ripples*.

"Earthquake!" Damien yells.

Turn to the next page.

You drop the diary and fall to the ground. But instead of a carpeted floor, you find yourself rolling in . . . dirt? Sunlight blinds you, and as you look around, you see the odd figure from Room XXXV running away, disappearing into distant shadows.

Then there is the *clang* of metal hitting metal, and a man wearing a helmet drops to the ground right in front of your face.

He looks quite dead.

Around you, a crowd roars. You stand up and brush yourself off. You are in the center of a coliseum. Not a modern sports coliseum, but an immense stone one. The building is magnificent, with rows of people rising up in all directions. You, Trent, and Damien are standing on the dirt floor of the arena.

There is a heap of bloodied bodies in the dirt in front of you. Near it, three men are fighting wildly, looking like any one of them could be next to fall. And it's not an even fight. A giant armed with a huge axe is attacking two men who have only small round shields and short swords.

"Those are gladiators," Damien says in wonderment. "Um, you guys? We're in a gladiator battle in the Roman Colosseum!"

A man with an eagle crest on his helmet barely manages to block a blow from the axe. He shouts at you, "Don't just stand there! Pick up a weapon and help, or you're next!"

Then something strikes you in the head and falls to the ground. It's a half-eaten pear. You turn and see a man in the front row shaking his fist at you. "Fight, cowards!" he yells.

Your ear stings, and it's sticky with pear juice. You don't know how or why this is happening, but this is REAL.

You've heard of how people get a "fight or flight" impulse in emergencies. And now, you understand what it means!

If you grab a weapon and fight, turn to page 74.

If you look for a way to escape, turn to page 142.

You scan around frantically for a way to escape the Colosseum's bloody melee. The arena is surrounded by a long, curved wall. You can see a large box of seats festooned with purple cloth. It's almost empty of spectators.

"FOLLOW ME!" you yell to Trent and Damien, and you start running toward the wall.

As you go, you pick up a long, light spear that was dropped by one of the slaughtered gladiators.

Holding the spear at shoulder level, you imagine your old track coach is speaking. "Take long strides for the pole vault, Astrid," Coach Kris would say. "Now, plant the butt end of the spear at the inner edge of the wall and drive your knee up! Great, now use your core muscles to move and turn—"

It's not pretty, but you make it over the wall! The spectators pull back in horror, as if you're some bloodthirsty monster instead of a girl from another century and continent. You can see vendors walking through the crowd, carrying trays holding cakes, dates, and meats. Others carry small cups of red wine.

Go on to the next page.

You turn to help the boys up, but neither one followed you. Instead, Damien and Trent are being chased around by the murderous giant while the crowd roars with laughter.

"Stop there!" yells someone very close. A guard seizes you, and you can't pull free.

The guard takes you to the fancy purple box seats. The people here wear expensive-looking clothes. A man in a fine toga lies on his side at the center, on a sort of love seat. He looks you over with amused interest.

"Well, girl, you are a curiosity," he says.

"My name is *Astrid*," you retort.

The guard shakes you roughly. "Shall I kill her, Caesar?" he asks.

Caesar sneezes, and speaks to his companions. "Astrid appeared in the Colosseum from nowhere, and then somehow vaulted out of the arena in a way which no gladiator has ever has done. Schedule her for another fight tomorrow."

As you are led away, your eyes search the arena, but you see no sign of the boys. Instead, to your horror, you see that Romans are flooding the arena with water! Gladiators are loading onto small ships to continue to battle.

You wonder how long you can survive as a Roman gladiator.

The End

You give Dentatus a look and cross your arms. "So, you would leave us that easily?"

The gladiator sees your determined expression and drops to a knee.

"Forgive me. Your arrival saved me from certain death in the Colosseum. I am only free because of you. Lead on, Astrid, into the sewer!"

You walk to the sewer's entry. The smell is *not* charming.

"I don't have time to explain," you say to the boys. "But this might get us back to Wisconsin."

Trent wrinkles his nose and steps back. "No *way* I'm going down there." You can't convince Trent to go any farther.

Go on to the next page.

You, Damien, and Dentatus step down the stairs into the murky light. The gladiator sees a man's stone face set in the stairway wall, and he bows to it.

"Thank you, Mercury, for keeping life interesting," says Dentatus.

At the base of the sewer stairs, tunnels branch off in different directions. Your eyes adjust to the dimness, and you spot the peculiar figure that beckoned to you bobbing down a tunnel on the left.

"This way!" You follow the shadowy figure down one tunnel and then another. Finally, after descending yet another stairway, you emerge into a cavernous room.

Turn to page 147.

You've caught up with the mysterious figure—but it's not *human*.

"Greetings!" the creature says in a voice like popcorn popping. "My name is <qh>, and I come from the star you humans call Betelgeuse. My apologies for accidentally bringing you here to this city from your past."

"So y-y-you're a time-traveling *alien*?" you stammer. It sounds like a dumb question, but it's always best to double-check these things.

"Correct," <qh> says. "But it is normal to be surprised by this news. After all, we are in a big galaxy, full of amazing things. Who could imagine a planet where the natives haven't eaten anything for 100,000 years because they're all on a diet?"

"Wow, is there a planet like that?" you ask.

"No, of course not!" pops <qh>. "Who could imagine it? Not me! Now, you should know that your Earth is unique across the galaxy in having so many different forms of life, from germs to redwood trees to whales. I am on a team of interplanetary zoologists. Our mission is to record the history of Earth's life and to preserve it. Sadly, in your time, Earth's wonderful animal and plant species are being driven to extinction with horrible speed."

Turn to the next page.

"Because of humans?" you ask.

"Yes! I've been working on a project to address this problem," <qh> explains, gesturing around the chamber. "Then I learned of a human who had learned how to journey through time: your Grandmother Dolores. She posed a problem, so I traveled to your Time Travel Inn using my equipment." One of <qh>'s arms points to a delicate crystal structure.

"While I was destroying your grandmother's technology, you burst into the room! I panicked and returned here to Rome, accidentally bringing you with me. So now I just need to return you home so I can finish my work."

You frown. "But what exactly is your project?"

<qh> hesitates. "Earth could be what you call 'a garden of Eden.' My job is to help that garden grow by *weeding* a few humans." The alien's laughter echoes in the chamber. "But don't worry! I am not working on a death ray! Instead, I'm developing a contagious and deadly virus that affects only your species."

"Well, that sucks," says Damien.

You get a sinking sensation. One way or another, you have to stop <qh> from destroying your own species!

If you try to persuade <qh> not to do this, turn to page 157.

If you choose to attack the alien to stop its plan, turn to page 160.

You glance back to the spot in the Great Sewer where the odd figure waved to you. But it's gone now, and the idea of returning underground right after being beneath the Colosseum doesn't sound good.

"Let's keep going to Spatula's villa," you agree. Carts, chariots, and people on horseback pass by on the road. Dentatus waves to a group of twenty strong-looking people and shouts: "Two litters, over here!"

Some men carry over two closed-up carriages on high platforms. You and Damien climb into one, and Dentatus and Trent take the other. Then the men lift the litters onto their shoulders and begin walking to your destination.

"How weird," you say, as the litter rocks you back and forth. "Why couldn't we just walk ourselves?"

"You know the old saying," answers Damien. "When in Rome, litter as the Romans do."

Two hours later, you are glad you didn't walk yourself. The city has begun to give way to a beautiful countryside. But as you pass through a wooded area, you hear a bloodcurdling scream.

Turn to the next page.

Someone yells, “Barbarians!” Then your litter lurches and falls to the ground, and the men who were carrying it sprint back down the road toward Rome.

A group of tough-looking men and women surround your two litters. They wear furs and carry swords. A wide man with a mammoth beard appears to be in charge.

“What is this?” he demands. “Only rich people use litters like these, but you sorry lot are anything but Roman nobles.”

As Dentatus politely explains your group’s story, Trent whispers, “I think these barbarians are Vandals and Goths.”

“Does that mean they’ll break all of our stuff and then play depressing music?” asks Damien.

The bearded barbarian is speaking. “So you’ve nothing to steal, and nothing to defend yourself with but wooden swords? What a waste of our time. Sadly, it’s still best to leave no witnesses.” The barbarians all laugh, and you get a chill. You step closer to Dentatus.

“There is no need to kill us!” you say. “We promise not to say a word.”

“That’s a promise you’ll keep,” says a voice. The barbarians open their ranks, and an old woman comes through. She pushes an uncorked leather bag in your hands. “Drink it,” she commands.

Go on to the next page.

Whatever's in the bag smells awful.

"Not thirsty," you say. But then the old woman holds a razor-sharp knife at your throat, so you drink. It's awful, like a smoothie of burnt mushrooms and raw chicken juice. After the old woman makes Damien, Trent, and Dentatus drink, the barbarians disappear back into the trees.

The four of you decide to keep walking to Spatula's villa. When you meet a girl leading a donkey, Dentatus tells her what happened.

"Oh, the barbarians used MCJ," she says.

"What's that?" Damien asks.

"Memory Cancelling Juice!" answers the girl. "It's a magical potion the pagan priests make to stop people from remembering."

You smile. "That's just superstition. I drank some, and my memory's fine. I can remember talking to Spatula, fighting in the Colosseum, and . . ." You realize that you can't remember anything before that.

Damien raises his eyebrows. "Astrid, don't joke around! You remember the Time Travel Inn, right?" Then he looks confused. "Wait, what were we just talking about?"

You shrug. "It must not have been very important. Anyway, when we get to the villa, I have dibs on picking the first room."

The End

152

Mercury raises his staff, and <qh> rushes to push a button that sends up a protective blue force field. As it appears, the force field holding your father vanishes.

Golden power streams from Mercury's staff. It hits <qh>'s force field and flows around it, destroying the equipment behind the alien. Vials and beakers break.

Go on to the next page.

"Useless god!" cries <qh>. "You've released my virus before it's ready! Now it will take thousands of years for it to mutate correctly."

As the alien and the god battle, Damien sneaks over to a fragile-looking part of the alien technology and begins hitting it with his wooden sword. "Please don't!" pops <qh>. "You might tear a hole in the time-space continuum!"

The whole chamber dips. The next thing you know, you fall through the air and land in snow.

Turn to page 155.

You're back in the parking lot of the Time Travel Inn! And so are Damien, Dentatus, and your father.

"Dad, we all made it back!" you yell, running toward him for a hug. "We changed history, and we're safe!"

Damien looks thoughtful. "I guess this raises three questions: Did we just go on an adventure or have a terrible experience? Were we using the time machine or was *it* using *us*? And what in the heck is *that*?"

He points to Room XXXV. There's a small, black rip in the air just above the doorway. It's pulling snowflakes into its blackness, and growing larger as you watch. You can feel the air around you sucking in toward it.

"That's the rip in time that <qh> warned us about!" you cry. "Dad, we need a ladder, and *fast*." Your father runs off, then returns with a ladder. You wave him to the basketball hoop mounted on the motel roof. He holds the ladder as you race up and pull out the basketball that's still stuck there behind the backboard.

Turn to the next page.

You look back at Room XXXV's doorway. The air is howling as it's sucked into the growing rip. Damien watches with you, and suddenly the rip starts pulling him. He whizzes through the snow toward the black hole.

Dentatus grabs Damien to stop him. You brace yourself and throw the basketball at the hole in time. The rip pulls the ball in. With a loud pop, the basketball plugs the rip like a cork!

The air quiets and the snow starts falling properly. As you watch, the rip in the air seems to heal itself around the outline of the basketball.

"Good pass, Astrid!" says Dad. "Since you fixed that rip, I guess we could call it a *stitch in time*." He is still laughing as a big SUV with snow tires pulls into the parking lot. A family gets out, and they seem normal except that they're all wearing surgical masks.

"Hey, what's with the masks?" asks Damien.

A girl wrestling a suitcase looks over. "They're for the pandemic! Where have YOU been?"

Dad looks at you. "Remember when <qh> said that his virus might take thousands of years to mutate? I think it's finally working!"

"Uh-oh. Hey, do you know where can we get some masks?" you ask the girl.

The End

What can you say to this alien that will change its mind? It seems intent on destroying humanity. But maybe you can use what <qh> said to persuade it not to.

"<qh>, you are the most intelligent being on this planet," you say. "Surely there's a wiser solution to our problem than simply destroying the human race? After all, life is precious."

"That is very civilized, Astrid," answers the alien. "And I do see *one* way out of this. You just have to travel in time and kill your grandmother before she invents her time machine."

"What?!" you exclaim. "I'm not killing my grandmother! True, she was never that nice to me, but murder seems like an overreaction." You think. "How about you send our group to different points in human history? Then we can teach humans in the past to be more environmentally responsible by warning them not to pollute the air or overfish. Just off the top of my head, I know we can save animals like the dodo, passenger pigeon, Tasmanian tiger—"

"Hey, the inventor Nikola Tesla knew fossil fuels were dangerous!" interrupts Damien. "Let's travel to 1870, before Thomas Edison worked on light bulbs. Then we can help Tesla work on efficient electricity and solar power to prevent climate change."

<qh> nods and starts making adjustments on the delicate machinery behind him. "It IS a good plan. Now stand a little closer together, please?"

"Where will you send us first?" asks Damien.

Turn to the next page.

"I'm sending you back to *your* time, but here in Rome," says <qh>, making adjustments on its time machine. "Then I'll finish working on my pandemic virus and release it here on the Roman Empire. You may notice a few changes when you arrive. Bye-bye!"

"Wait!" you shout. "What about—"

There is a sudden shift, and the sewer system disappears. You're standing in the ruins of Ancient Rome, and now they truly ARE ancient. The Colosseum is covered in vines, and the sounds of insects, birds, and animals fill the air. Down the avenue, you see a herd of gigantic woolly rhinos.

Three hyenas round the corner of a deserted building and spot your group. The hyenas instantly charge, but then veer away at the last moment. As the hyenas trot off, you notice a group of extraterrestrials watching you.

"Were the humans in danger, Mother?" asks a little salamander alien.

"No," the larger alien says. "They are the rarest species on Earth, and are well protected. But they are also the most *dangerous* species, so we keep them in this time and place."

"Let's look at the wooly rhinos next!" says the child.

As the group walks off, you realize that you are the last humans left on Earth. And you're the star attractions in a wildlife park for aliens.

The End

“You think you can destroy humankind?” you demand of <qh>. You draw the wooden sword you were given at the Colosseum. “Well, we’re going to stop you by doing a little weeding of our own!”

You leap forward and smash the sword down on the top of what would be <qh>’s head. But the weapon simply splinters to bits, and <qh> gives a complicated shrug with its many shoulders.

“This human said the same thing to me when *he* traveled back in time to stop me,” says <qh>. The alien points with an arm, and a shimmering blue barrier appears in the corner. Behind it is your father.

“Dad!” you cry out, rushing to him. When you hit the blue barrier, it feels like you hit a wall of cold slime, and you pulse back into the room.

Dentatus raises his arms to the sky, calling out, “Oh, Mercury, pride of Olympus, brightly shining among the gods. You stitched together the stars in the void of space, and from them has come this unpleasant being. Hear my prayer and give assistance to your undeserving follower.”

A hush falls over the chamber. Then the air rushes in your ears and a tall, glowing man appears in the center of the room.

Turn to page 162.

"Mercury!" gasps Dentatus.

The god laughs, and it sounds like hot honey in your ears.

"Cool!" says Damien. "But isn't that Hermes, not Mercury?"

Dentatus gestures for silence. "Hermes is the Greek name for the god of messengers, thieves, and merchants. But we Romans call him Mercury. Now, quiet!"

"I have come from atop Mount Olympus down to the Great Sewer, so it's already quite a day," says Mercury. He looks at <qh> and frowns. "This child from the stars has wandered far from home!"

Turn to page 152.

You look at the kindergarteners with surprise. They could have returned home any time, but stayed because they were dinosaur-crazy?!

It's obvious that you have to get these children back to their parents. But at the same time, you need to find your own mom and dad. Then you get an idea.

"Hey, you guys love dinosaurs, right?" you ask the children. "Then you must know that different dinosaurs lived at different times. So let's take a field trip and see some new dinosaurs, okay?"

The kids love this, and immediately hold hands and crowd closer as you make adjustments on the time machine. You look at Damien and say, "Call their parents." Then you hit the power button and run. You hope that if you can get far enough away, you won't be swept back to modern times with the children.

Turn to the next page.

164

Your plan works! Faith and the other kindergarteners are gone, and Damien can help return them home. As you mentally pat yourself on the back, a woman with long gray hair and piercing eyes appears out of thin air. Davy Cricket makes a happy chittering sound. He leaps off your shoulder and bounds toward her. You stare in astonishment at the gray-haired woman. "Grandmother Dolores!" you cry out. "I found you!"

"Hello, Astrid," your long-lost grandmother says, giving you the briefest hug. "And *I* found *you*, along with this naughty *Archaboilus*. What kind of mischief have you been up to, Davy?"

You feel strangely shy seeing your grandmother after all this time. But you give her a brief report of your arrival at her inn, your adventures so far, and your scheme to trick the kindergarteners into going home again.

Turn to page 166.

166

Grandmother Dolores listens approvingly. "Sending those children home for their own safety was probably the right thing to do. I'm sending you back home for the same reasons. Stay put there while I sort out this Doomsday Event."

"W-what?!" you sputter with anger. "My whole family moved from Florida because you disappeared. Both of my parents are gone, looking for you. Plus, a kid got eaten!"

"Good points," admits Grandmother Dolores. "But let me explain something. You're made of atoms that are millions of years old, and all of those atoms also exist *here*, in the past. So if you stay, the atoms you're made of have to coexist with the atoms that are already present. Since atoms can't be in *two* places at once, you'll explode!"

Go on to the next page.

You cross your arms. "But if that's true, why didn't the kindergarteners blow up?"

Grandmother smiles. "Maybe you *are* smart enough to stay here. But we must leave right now." She tinkers with a small chrome and crystal device and adds, "Hang on."

The jungle ripples and the ground lurches. Then you smell salt and man's voice calls out, "Unfurl those starboard sails and be quick about it!"

You're on board a sailing ship—and it's flying a black pirate flag!

"Where are we?" you whisper. "And *why*?"

"Get down!" says your grandmother, crouching to avoid the opening sails. You follow her lead. She waves you to follow her to a small door. She opens the door into a dark, narrow hallway.

"We're on a pirate ship in the Caribbean Sea in 1720," says Grandmother. "The reason we're here is because my calculations show that just after your 'modern day' back at the Time Travel Inn, time just *stops*. I call that time stoppage the Doomsday Event."

Turn to the next page.

Following your grandmother down the narrow passage, you whisper, "Why not just go to the future to see what happens?"

Grandmother takes down two cutlasses from the wall and hands one to you. "Because it's impossible to see something that hasn't happened yet! But in my investigations, I've learned a man is linked to the Doomsday Event. He's a twentieth-century mathematician who's traveled through time many times, always escaping me in the process. And that villain is on this ship, *now*." She tests the edge of her blade with her thumb. "If I'm right, he's insane, evil, and a genius. Now, you look for his cabin that way, and I'll go over here."

Grandmother points you down a hall and then disappears. *Great*, you think. *I'm supposed to handle a time-lord pirate-captain-genius with an oversized butter knife.*

You creep down the hall and look through an open door. A man with wild gray hair sits with his back to you, writing furiously. You sidle in to peek over his shoulder. He's crossing items off a list:

~~Freejack Grogmaster~~
~~Captain Scab~~
~~Scurvyskivvies Malloy~~
Horatio Magellan Einstein

The floorboard creaks beneath you. The man leaps to his feet. He looks familiar, and you see that he has a huge mustache. "Drop the blade before I cut you in half!" he commands in a German accent.

If you swing your cutlass, turn to page 112.

If you do as he says and drop your blade, turn to page 173.

You know that you have to stop the Blue Wizards from taking over the city and slaughtering its people.

"The Blue Wizards' sorcery is impressive!" you announce loudly. "But where I come from, there is *another* kind of magick."

The Grey Council rustles around, and the Blue Wizards are staring at you as if you've grown a second head.

"And just what is this 'magick'?" asks Ramsteen skeptically.

"It's called Peer Mediation," you reply, as you mentally review the rules of conflict resolution from your old school. "Here's how it works: First, I ask someone to help me begin. Today, that person will be Ramsteen. Now, everybody give him a hand!"

You start clapping and give Trent and Damien a look. The boys clap too. Slowly, the members of the Grey Council join in. The Blue Wizards hesitate. They don't want to seem as if they're insulting Ramsteen, so finally they also join the applause.

"I really appreciate your coming in today," you tell the assembled wizards. "The work we're going to do will help us get along and feel good about ourselves."

Turn to the next page.

Ramsteen frowns. "Conquering Zamora *was* making me feel good about myself."

"Yes, but perhaps that feeling is connected to anger stemming from something else," you answer. "Now, to build empathy, I want you to remember when you were in a vulnerable place. Maybe you can remember something slightly embarrassing that happened when you were a child. Let's say, before you were nine years old. Maybe you got on the wrong bus home on the first day of school, or or—yes, Damien, what is it?"

Damien puts his hand down and excitedly tells the group about a time when his trumpet had a broken spit valve in band.

"Okay," you say, playing along. "Is there something the other students could have done to make you feel better about this situation?"

Damien thinks. "It would've been nice if someone had helped me mop up the puddle."

You quickly move on, giving the Greys and Blues tips on how to use Peer Mediation to help each other. The tips include steps like:

—Listening to everyone.

—Being calm.

—Not trying to fix things or give advice.

—Asking open-ended questions.

Go on to the next page.

"Now, let's practice," you say. "Are you ready for some role-playing?"

"Are those the magick spells?" asks Lamonta.

"Sort of," you say, then you cup a hand to your ear. "Now, are you ready for some role-playing? Because *I can't heeaaarrrr you!"*

The wizards reluctantly agree that they are ready.

"Good! Now Ramsteen, did you think of your embarrassing incident yet?"

The Blue Wizard sighs. "When I was nine, I brought a gift that I was ashamed of to my friend's birthday party." He looks a little sad, so you walk over to him with a concerned look.

"Are you okay?"

"Sure," he grunts. But he doesn't say any more.

You look at the wizards. "Do you see what I did wrong? I asked Ramsteen a *closed* question with a yes or no answer. I'll try asking an open question: Ramsteen, your face is so sad. I wonder why that is?"

To your amazement, a tear slides down the wizard's cheek. "It's my parents," he sobs. "They've been putting pressure on me to invade Z-Z-Zamora for years! And to make it happen, I've done things I'm not proud of: plundering, marauding, burning, and even occasionally turning someone into a raccoon for no good reason."

You nod and keep speaking quietly with the wizard. But you don't try to talk him out of invading Zamora. Instead, you let Ramsteen talk *himself* out of it.

Turn to the next page.

The Blue Wizards quietly leave after that, and Lamonta approaches you.

"Peer Mediation is powerful magick, but it is not pleasant to watch. In fact, while it saved Zamora today, I never want to hear of Peer Mediation again. May I send you back to Earth? Please say yes, and promise not to ever ask me why *I* look sad."

You look at the boys and nod. Lamonta then begins drawing sigils on the stone floor with her staff, and the next thing you know, you're back in the basement under the Time Travel Inn.

"I guess people don't talk about their feelings much on Zamora," you shrug.

"Yeah, and it was *awesome*," says Trent.

The End

You set your cutlass on the desk, as the Captain asked.

"I'm not here to hurt anyone. What's that list you're writing?"

The Captain hesitates, then drops his own blade.

"I'm trying to come up with a proper pirate name. But never mind that. From your clothing, I can see that you're from the future. What are you doing here?"

He knows! Despite Grandmother's warning, you quickly tell him your whole story. A moment later, four pirates escort Grandmother into the room. "We caught a stowaway, Captain," says one.

"Good heavens!" Grandmother Dolores cries. "The person trying to destroy the world is Albert Einstein?!"

So THAT'S why he looks so familiar, you think.

Albert Einstein looks confused. "I don't want to destroy the *world*. I just want to do a little plundering and looting. And who are *you*?"

Grandmother folds her arms. "I'm Dr. Dolores Alcindor, an inventor from the twenty-first century. But I must know your story. Why have *you* traveled to so many different points in history?"

Turn to the next page.

174

Einstein laughs. "Because I love to travel! I don't have many hobbies, and that's my favorite one."

The world's most famous scientist explains that he'd gotten bored with coming up with new equations year after year.

"Yes, my work showed that a person reaching the speed of light could *theoretically* travel to the future," says Einstein. "But I wanted something practical. So I researched time-traveling to the past, and to my shock, I succeeded at it. Since I've always loved pirate stories, I've decided to become a pirate myself. When people talk about famous pirates, their names will be Captain Kidd, Blackbeard, and the feared Horatio Magellan *Einstein*."

He sips from a mug and winces. "The worst part of being a pirate is the grog. It's awful stuff."

"But won't your actions change history?" you ask.

Einstein sets his mug down. "Think of the past as a finished painting. You can't erase that paint, but you can paint *over* it. That's what I'm doing. The old paint of history is still there, but now there are two paintings on the same canvas. In the old painting, I'm a famous scientist. In the new one, I'm a fearsome pirate."

Go on to the next page.

Grandmother Dolores frowns. "But none of this explains the Doomsday Event!"

She and Einstein then get into a complex discussion about math and time. It's awkward, because you can barely follow what they're saying, and the four pirates are completely lost.

In the end, Grandmother and Einstein decide that mathematical equations only make it *seem* as if time will end in a Doomsday Event.

"This just shows the limits of our equations," Einstein says. "In other words, the problem is with our math, not the universe."

"So we don't need to prevent the end of the world?" You feel strangely disappointed.

"Apparently, there is no end of the world," says Grandmother Dolores. "But I need to get back to my research to prove it." She pulls out her portable time machine, and, as Grandmother tinkers with it, you wave. "Happy plundering, Captain Horatio Magellan Einstein."

Turn to the next page.

The world's most famous scientist beams and raises his mug—and then the ship's cabin shimmers, and you are suddenly back in the lobby of the Time Travel Inn.

"Astrid!" Your mother races around the counter and hugs you fiercely. "When your friend Damien brought back those kindergarteners, I was worried sick. And if I'd known she was with *you*, Dolores, I would have worried even more! We have literally been looking EVERYWHERE for you." Mom takes a deep breath. "Anyway, welcome home to both of you."

You hug your mother back, but your mind is still spinning with everything that's just happened. You turn back to your grandmother.

"Was what Einstein said about the painting true?" you ask. "Can we really go anywhere in history and do anything we want, Grandma Dolores? Grandma . . . Dolores?"

But there's no one standing beside you anymore. You may be safe and sound back at the Time Travel Inn, but your Grandmother Dolores has vanished again.

The End

Looking at the children's smiles, you decide not to make them go home right away. But you can't let them stay here with the dinosaurs; it's just too dangerous. Davy Cricket shifts on your shoulder, reminding you of something.

"How did you kids know Davy Cricket's name?"

"He belongs to the old lady," says a little boy whose name tag reads "Zach."

"Does she have long, gray hair?" you ask.

"Yes! She sometimes uses words that seem mean. But she says she's just being honest, so if it hurts your feelings, that's your problem."

"That's my Grandmother Dolores, all right!"

The children explain that Grandmother checks in with them now and then with her time machine.

"She had to leave in a hurry last time and told us to watch Davy Cricket. But then *he* disappeared, and we didn't know where he was until we saw you."

You look at Davy Cricket. "You used the kids' time machine to go to the Time Travel Inn, right?"

The giant cricket chirps, which you take as a "yes."

Damien whispers to you. "Astrid, I just got a great idea. Let's travel to when Leonardo da Vinci paints the *Mona Lisa*. We'll take the painting, bring it back to our time, and sell it for millions of dollars!"

You shake your head. "How would two kids sell a priceless painting?"

"Etsy!"

Turn to the next page.

"Damien, if the painting was fresh, an art expert would ask why it wasn't old! Now repeat after me: We can't mess up the past, or we'll mess up the future, which is our present."

Damien cocks his head like a dog trying to understand a new command. "Huh?"

You sigh and turn to the kindergarteners.

"Who wants to go on some field trips?" you ask them. The children all love the idea, so you explain that your group will just dip in and out of history for short visits while you look for signs of Grandmother Dolores or your parents.

You gather the kids, have them hold hands, and turn on the time machine. Then you all GO!!!! Over the next few hours, your group sees:

- Herds of gigantic mastodons stretching as far as you can see
- A sabretooth tiger sleeping in the sun and snoring like a chainsaw
- Menominee hunters wearing tanned deerskin clothing
- French fur traders playing cards on a stump
- A forest fire so intense, you can feel the air around you being sucked into the flames
- A woman changing a flat tire on what must be Wisconsin's first car

Go on to the next page.

But despite all your travels through time, there's no Grandmother Dolores! By now, the children are yawning and obviously need naps. So for the final trip, you set the time to the present.

Your group materializes inside Room 1. To your shock, the children are barely surprised. You quickly unlock some more rooms and offer beds for them to nap in.

It's still snowing outside as you go to the lobby and use the phone there to call the local elementary school. Soon, emotional parents pull into the parking lot and tearful reunions take place.

A local television reporter and a camera person corner you. "I'm here with Astrid Alcindor, who just moved to Wisconsin from Florida. On her first day here, she's somehow managed to solve a mystery that had thrown this community into turmoil: the missing kindergarten class of H.G. Wells Elementary School! Astrid, you are a hero to these parents. How does that make you feel?"

"Oh, I'm not a hero," you say, blushing. "The real hero is—

"*Me*," says Damien, stepping in front of you.

The End

You glare at Trent. “Fine,” you say.

Damien steps forward and puts his hands on the device.

“On three, Trent and I will both let go,” you say. “Ready? One . . . two . . . three.”

To your surprise, Trent releases his grip, so you do too. Damien steps back with the machine. “See?” he says. “That wasn’t so hard.” You spot a smaller device on the desk that looks like the one Damien is holding. As you pick it up, you hear Damien say, “Hey, I wonder what this button does?”

Then the whole room tilts sideways, and disappears!

You and the boys are standing outside, and you’re surrounded by trees. But the snow is gone, and the air is warm and buzzing with insects.

“Damien? What’d you do?” demands Trent.

Damien shrugs innocently. “All I did was press a button!” Meanwhile, Davy Cricket is up on his shoulder, his antennae waving in curiosity.

You hear voices in the distance, so you follow the sound to a nearby stream. There, you see two men in old-timey clothing digging in the soil by the water.

Go on to the next page.

"You guys, we just traveled back in time!" you whisper. "Now be *really* careful. Have you ever read that science fiction story where a guy time-travels to the age of dinosaurs, but while he's there, he accidentally steps on a butterfly? That tiny change affects the future so much, when the guy returns to his own time, the United States has a different president."

"Fine, no stepping on butterflies," says Trent. "But what about giant crickets?"

"Don't move, ya durned gold thieves, or I'll plug ya!" A man in old-fashioned clothes is pointing a rifle at you. Davy Cricket hides inside Damien's jacket. The man then forces you and the boys down to his companions, who are shoveling up rocks glinting with gold.

The miners listen suspiciously as you say, "We're newcomers here, and came this way by accident."

"By the way, what year is it?" asks Damien.

One of the gold miners spits chewing tobacco juice in the stream. "It's still 1900, I reckon," he says. "But the only part of your tale I believe is that y'all are strangers to these parts. Cuz if you knew what we do to thieves, you wouldn't have come."

Turn to the next page.

The men all laugh. You don't like the sound of it one bit. You look down at the small device that you brought from the inn. It looks like a remote control. It has one big button, and a digital readout on the side that says "1900." Using adjusters, you change the date to the present day. Then you stand closer to the boys. "Get ready," you say, and you press the button.

The forest starts to dim, and the man with the rifle cries out, "They're getting away!" A gunshot rings out.

But you're back in the motel room. You run to the door and go outside. It's still snowing, and your dad's van is right there in the parking lot.

You're relieved until Trent says, "Those idiot miners didn't even notice me taking this." He holds up one of their golden rocks.

"What did you do?" you shout. Trent didn't listen to *anything you said about not disrupting the past!*

"It's probably nothing but fool's gold," Damien says.

"Um, you guys?" You point up to where the basketball hoop was. But where it used to be, there's a soccer ball stuck in the roof's gutter.

"What?" Trent asks you. "*You're* the one who kicked it up there. You missed the goal by a mile." And sure enough, there's now a soccer net in the parking lot where one wasn't before.

Go on to the next page.

You look around as the snow silently falls. It all seems so peaceful and normal, it's hard to believe that something's now very, very wrong.

You glance at the sign for the motel and read "Back Inn Time."

"Wait, this place was called the Time Travel Inn before!" you cry out. "And Trent, don't you remember, we were playing basketball? I stole the basketball and dunked it? But now we've changed the future! What else did we change?"

But Trent and Damien are just staring at you like you've lost your mind. And you are shocked to realize that now you like soccer more than you like basketball. When did *that* happen? Oh well, maybe this world will be better than the last one.

"I'm going to go find a ladder," you say. "And then I seriously have to track down my parents."

The End

ABOUT THE ARTIST

María Pesado is an illustrator from Barcelona, Spain. After graduating in Graphic Arts and Illustration, she worked as a decorative painter, muralist, and teacher in art workshops. Her paintings have been shown at several exhibitions, and she has directed multi-disciplinary events of illustration and scenic arts. In the editorial field, she has published illustrated children's books, and she is currently making her way into comics, collaborating with sci-fi and horror magazines. She lives with her partner, by the sea, and loves books and fantasy movies.

ABOUT THE AUTHOR

You look at the photo and think, "Now *that's* a big book." Then you realize this is a biography of **Bart King**. You assume he must be the author of the book you're holding. After all, Bart wrote 30 other titles, including a science-fiction novel called *The Drake Equation*. But the truth is more interesting. Two years ago, Bart was out hiking in a forest when he heard a loud *pop.* To his surprise, a printed manuscript had appeared on the trail in front of him! Naturally, Bart picked it up.

If you want to read the story that Bart discovered on the trail that day, turn to page 1.

If you would like to learn more about Bart's extraordinary life, turn to page 267.

For games, activities, and other fun stuff, or to write to Bart King, visit us online at CYOA.com

CHOOSE YOUR OWN ADVENTURE®

THE CITADEL OF WHISPERS

KAZIM ALI

"Several challenging and compelling stories to explore, and YA readers will love them all."

–Wil Wheaton, *Stand By Me*, *Big Bang Theory*

AN EPIC INTERACTIVE FANTASY

ENTER THE WORLD OF ELARIA. YOU are Krishi, a Whisperer studying ancient, secret magic at the Citadel. A secret visitor arrives late one night with news of the encroaching attack by the powerful Narbolin empire, who are poised to possess all of the kingdom of Elaria. Will the decisions you make protect the many wondrous people of this rich, fantastic world?

KAZIM ALI was born in the UK to parents of Indian descent. He is the writer of over 20 books of poetry and prose, and he is currently professor and chair of the Department of Literature at the University of California San Diego.

WWW.CYOA.COM

ONI
PRESS

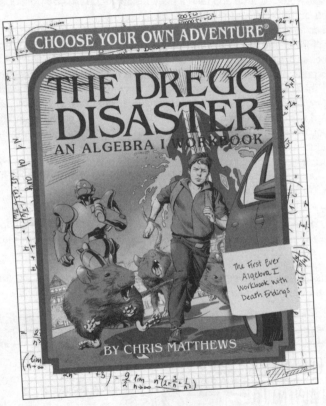

CHAPTER 1

Walking home from soccer practice, there's so much on your mind that you almost go right by it. But the metal clasp catches your eye in the evening sun. It's a woman's clutch wallet, an old one, lying on the ground. Someone must have dropped it here on the sidewalk. You pick it up and take a peek inside. It contains 35 dollars, a couple of old receipts and a restaurant punch-card for Wong's Deli.

Whoever left their wallet is one punch away from a free sandwich.

You dig further and find what looks like a strange access card. It's shiny and metallic, with a blue, stylized "D". You would recognize *that* logo anywhere. It belongs to the Dregg Corporation. Their main research facility is here in town, but they have subsidiaries and shell companies all over the world. They make chemicals, pharmaceuticals, kids toys, military supplies, snack foods plus they manage a bunch of oil refineries.

The card is small but heavy for its size. And it's not a regular Dregg employee ID because you'd recognize that. Your mom used to be a Product Manager there, until her Korean skincare website took off. No, this card is for something else.

You turn it over. There's a small holographic ID of a woman in a lab coat and the name Dr. Donda LaBella underneath. Under that are the words: IF FOUND PLEASE RETURN TO THE DREGG CORPORATION. $1000 REWARD.

Note to the reader: On most pages of this story, you will be given a choice, and in order to find the next page in the story, you will need to use your math skills!

For this first page, solve the problem below and when you find a solution, go to the page that matches your answer!

You have some Dregg Donuts at home. You have 3 unopened boxes, plus four extras. In total, there are 43 donuts. How many donuts come in a box?

Continue to the page that matches your solution (13)

CHAPTER 1

Check your work: you should have arrived here from page 1

Note to the reader: Thirteen donuts! A baker's dozen! Great work on navigating this book so far. At the top of this page is a grey box with a dotted border. Use these boxes to check your work. If you solved the problem on "page 1" and got a solution that brought you here, you are off to a great start! Good luck as the choices (and the math problems) get harder!

That settles that! A thousand bucks reward money? Hello e-bike.

But how should you return the card and wallet? You could go straight to Dregg Tower and hand it in at Security. Or you could try finding Dr. Donda LaBella directly. She might be grateful enough to give you a bonus. This card is obviously valuable.

Note to the reader: This time, there is a choice! Decide which path you want to follow, and solve the problem that goes with that choice. Your solution will take you to your next page!

If you want return the wallet and strange glowing card to Dregg Tower ...
Solve the following proportion for x

$$\frac{x}{15} = \frac{21}{7}$$

Continue to the page that matches your solution (45)

If you decide to look for the wallet's owner (What kind of name is Donda LaBella anyway?), turn to page... Solve the following proportion for x

$$\frac{x}{14} = \frac{10}{5}$$

Continue to the page that matches your solution (28)

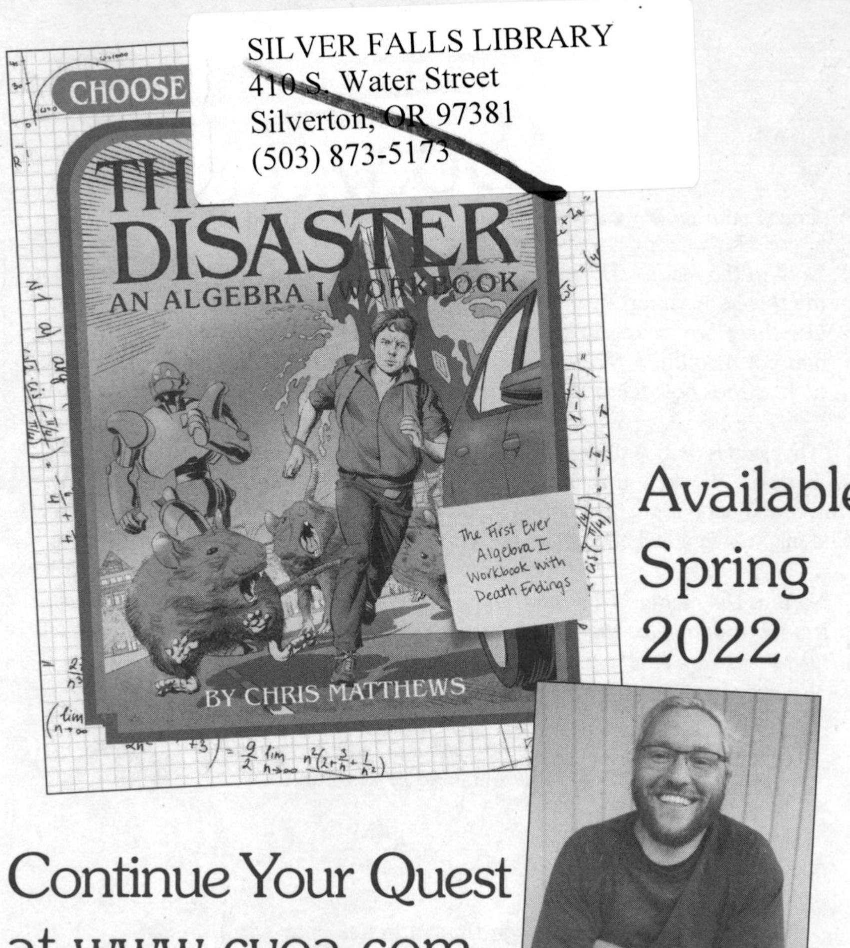
CHOOSE
DISASTER
AN ALGEBRA I WORKBOOK
The First Ever Algebra I Workbook with Death Endings
BY CHRIS MATTHEWS

Available
Spring
2022

Continue Your Quest at www.cyoa.com

ABOUT CHRIS MATTHEWS

Chris Matthews is a middle-school math teacher from Spokane, Washington and he has been working in Denver and Seattle classrooms for ten years. He loves working with students and creating games that encourage mathematical exploration. When he is not teaching or writing, Chris spends time climbing, biking, and watching bad movies.

Chris earned his Masters in Education from Seattle Pacific University in 2020, and he is an alumnus of Bike & Build, Americorps NCCC, Western Washington University, NOLS and YMCA Camp Reed. The Dregg Disaster is his first publication.